79

3 2010
2010

010

0
12

THE SPANISH
GROOM

THE SPANISH GROOM

BY

LYNNE GRAHAM

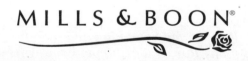

MILLS & BOON®

MILLS & BOON and
MILLS & BOON with the Rose Device
are registered trademarks of the publisher.

First published in Great Britain 1999
Large Print edition 1999
Harlequin Mills & Boon Limited,
Eton House, 18-24 Paradise Road,
Richmond, Surrey TW9 1SR

© Lynne Graham 1999

ISBN 0 263 16170 6

Set in Times Roman 15¾ on 16½ pt
16-9909-59079 C1

Printed and bound in Great Britain
by Antony Rowe Ltd, Chippenham, Wiltshire

CHAPTER ONE

CÉSAR replaced the phone, his lean, strong face taut, wide, sensual mouth compressed. So Jasper's health was failing. Since his godfather was eighty-two, the news should not have come as a shock...

Rising restively from behind his desk, César crossed his spacious office—a contemporary triumph of glass and steel, wholly in keeping with a minimalist building much mentioned in architectural digests. Formed round a series of stylish atriums embellished with lush greenery and tranquil fountains, the office block César had commissioned to house the London headquarters of the Valverde Mercantile Bank was as elegant and impressive as its owner.

But César was indifferent to his surroundings. His thoughts were on Jasper Dysart, who had become his guardian when he was twelve. He was a true English eccentric, a bachelor bookworm who had made rare butterflies his lifestudy, and the kindest old man imaginable. César and Jasper were mental poles apart. Indeed César and Jasper might as well have come from different planets, but César was fond of Jasper, and suddenly grimly aware that the only thing Jasper had ever wanted him to do remained undone and time now seemed to be running out...

A knock on the door heralded the entrance of his executive assistant, Bruce Gregory. Normally the very epitome of confident efficiency, for some reason Bruce chose to hover, a sheet of paper rather tensely clutched between his fingers.

'Yes?' César prompted impatiently.

The young blond man cleared his throat. 'The random security check has turned up a member of staff with financial problems.'

'You know the rules. Getting into debt is grounds for instant dismissal.' César frowned at the need to make this reminder when that warning appeared in all staff employment contracts. 'We deal with too much confidential information to take the risk.'

Bruce grimaced. 'This...er...person is a very minor cog in the bank, César.'

'I still don't see a problem.' The brilliant dark eyes were cool, unemotional, the hallmark of a hugely successful financial genius with neither time nor sympathy for those who broke the rules. César was contemptuous of weakness, and ruthless at exploiting it in business opponents.

'Actually...it's Dixie.'

César stilled. Bruce studied the wall, not wanting to see César smile at that information. Everybody know how César felt about Dixie Robinson, currently the equivalent of an office junior on the top floor. Dixie, quite simply, irritated the hell out of César.

She had not one single trait which *didn't* grate on her cool, sophisticated employer. In recent weeks, César had been heard to censure her sloppy appearance, her clumsiness, her friendly chatter, her constant collecting for obscure charities...and, it had to be admitted, a degree of incompetence at business skills that had raised her to the level of an office mascot. César, alone, was deflatingly untouched by the compensatingly warm and caring personality which made Dixie so universally well liked.

But then on a level playing field, Dixie Robinson would never have got as far as an interview at the Valverde Mercantile Bank: she had no qualifications. Jasper Dysart had *asked* César to give her a job. Personnel had jumped to the task, only to find themselves seriously challenged by Dixie's inability to cope with technology. Passed on from one department to another, Jasper's protegée had finally arrived on the top floor, a fact which had delighted her elderly sponsor but which had unfortunately brought Dixie into César's immediate radius.

César extended a hand for the computer print-out. Bruce passed it over with perceptible reluctance.

Scanning down the sheet, César slowly elevated a winged ebony brow. Evidently Dixie Robinson led a double life. The list of her dissatisfied creditors included a well-known interior designer and the kind of bills that indicated some serious alcoholic partying. César was tickled pink, his even white teeth flashing in a derisive grin of satisfaction.

So her resolutely innocent front *was* a façade, just as he had always suspected it was. For a split second he thought how appalled Jasper would be—Jasper who broke out with a modest sherry only at Christmas and who fondly believed that Dixie Robinson was a thoroughly decent, old-fashioned girl with homely tastes.

'Obviously she's been really stupid. But if she's sacked, she'll sink like a stone,' Bruce pointed out gruffly. 'She doesn't handle anything confidential, César—'

'She has access.'

'I don't really think she's bright enough to use that kind of information,' Bruce breathed tautly.

César gave him a look of grim amusement. 'Got you fooled as well, has she?'

'Fooled?' Bruce's brow furrowed.

'Now I know why she always looks half asleep—too many late nights.'

In desperation, Bruce shot his last bolt in Dizzy's defence. 'I guess Mr Dysart will be upset not to find her here on his next visit.'

'Jasper's not well. It's unlikely that he'll be in London in the near future.'

'I'm sorry to hear that.' Bruce studied his employer's coolly uninformative face warily. Well, that was that, he acknowledged. He couldn't say he was surprised either. César was not a soft touch. And proof of such foolish extravagance had merely increased his contempt. 'I'll pass the information concerning Dixie on to Personnel.'

'No. I'll deal with this personally,' César contradicted without warning.

Bruce wasn't quite fast enough to hide his dismay.

'I'll see Miss Robinson at four,' César completed.

'She'll be very upset, César.'

'I think I can handle it,' César drawled, in the sort of tone that made the younger man flush and go into retreat.

Alone again, César studied that list of creditors, a smouldering look awakening in his narrowed gaze. Jasper was very fond of little Dixie Robinson. In fact, superficially Dixie was exactly the kind of young woman Jasper longed to have

César produce as the future Mrs Valverde, the sort of girl who didn't intimidate an innocent old bachelor totally out of step with a world approaching the Millenium.

So there it was, out in the open. The admission that he *had* disappointed his godfather, César conceded with exasperated reluctance. Jasper's deepest and most naive hope had always been that César would marry, settle down and have a family. And live happily ever after, of course, César affixed, scornfully recalling his late parents. His volatile Italian mother and equally volatile Spanish father had between them stacked up half a dozen failed marriages before dying young and anything but happy.

Wincing at the very idea of marital togetherness with any woman, but with his conscience still causing him rare discomfiture, César brooded on the problem of Jasper's disappointment. Experience had taught César that there was no such thing as a problem without a solution. When shorn of the inhibiting factors of emotion and morality, the impossible could almost always become the possible...

No doubt Jasper fondly imagined that his veiled hints about what a wonderful wife Dixie Robinson would make some fortunate male had been too subtle to be recognised for what they were. In point of fact, Jasper had the subtlety of a sledgehammer, and when César had first picked up on his godfather's pointed comments on the subject of his protegée he had been anything but amused.

But now César grimly acknowledged that were he to announce that he *had* got engaged to Dixie Robinson, Jasper would be overjoyed. César visualised Dixie with something less than joy, but Jasper thought the sun rose and set on her. And, as pleasing Jasper was César's only goal, there would be little point in persuading any other woman into playing his temporary fiancée. What Jasper wanted, César decided there and then, Jasper deserved to receive.

As he pictured how he might sensibly stress the need for a lengthy engagement between two such disparate personalities as himself and the office klutz, César began warming to the exercise. It would make Jasper happy. And Jasper, who could spend hours just choosing a single book, would scarcely expect his godson to leap straight from an engagement into matrimony.

And Dixie Robinson? Dixie was between a rock and a hard place. She would do as she was told. Around him, she was quiet and cowed, which was just as well because César was convinced he would strangle her if she behaved any other way. He would slim her down, smarten her up, do whatever it took to ensure that the fake engagement appeared credible. He would be nothing less than thorough...

'At f-four?' Dixie stammered, pale as milk as she stood over the photocopier, striving somewhat hopelessly to conceal the 'inoperative' sign flashing above a pile of discarded photocopies printed with impossibly tiny type. 'But why would Mr Valverde want to see me?'

Already conscious that his attempt to speak up on her behalf had taxed César's patience, Bruce did not dare utter a word of warning.

'Is it about that Arab guy whose call I cut off?'

Bruce tensed. 'He doesn't know about that.'

'That file I accidentally took out?'

Bruce paled at the reminder. 'You got it back from the bus company.'

Dixie gulped. 'I've been trying so hard to stay out of Mr Valverde's way...it's just he keeps on popping up in the most unexpected places.'

'César likes to be visible. What sort of unexpected places?' Bruce could not resist asking.

'Like the kitchen...when I was icing the cake for Jayne's leaving party last week. Mr Valverde went through the roof,' Dixie recounted, half under her breath, shuddering at the recollection. 'He asked me if I thought I was working in a bakery and I ended up spelling her name wrong. Then yesterday he walked into that little room the cleaning staff use and found me asleep…he gave me the biggest fright of my life!'

'César expects all his employees to make a special effort to stay awake between nine and five,' Bruce responded, deadpan.

Currently working two jobs just to keep a roof over her head, Dixie gave him an abstracted look, her eyes, so dark a blue they were violet, strained with anxiety and tiredness. Fear emanated from her in waves. Small though she was, she seemed to grow even smaller as she hunched her shoulders and bowed her head, the explosive mop of her long curly dark brown hair falling over her softly rounded face. She was terrified of César Valverde, had become acquainted with every hiding place on the executive floor within days of arriving there.

But then she had started out on the wrong foot, hadn't she? Her big mouth, she conceded glumly. While covering for the receptionist during her afternoon break, Dixie had begun chatting to the gorgeous blonde seated in the waiting area. In an effort to make entertaining conversation, she had mentioned the world-famous model, Mr Valverde had entertained on his yacht the previous weekend. And then her employer had strolled out of the lift…

And without the slightest warning all hell had broken loose! The blonde, who it later transpired had actually been waiting for César Valverde, had risen to her feet to throw a jealous fit of outrage and accuse him of being a 'love-rat'.

Dixie's co-workers had very decently acknowledged that that charge might well have some basis in fact, but it was not an allegation César had expected to face within the hallowed portals of the bank because one of his own staff had been recklessly indiscreet. Indeed what César had had to say about Dixie's gossiping tongue had been, as one of the directors had frankly admitted while trying hard not to smile, unrepeatable. Since then she had been banned from manning Reception.

'Is César dating any nice girls at present?' Jasper always asked hopefully in his letters to Dixie, not seeming to appreciate that at the threat of what his godfather deemed a 'nice girl' César Valverde would undoubtedly run a mile. It was a well-worn joke in the bank that César's answer to commitment was escape.

But Dixie's troubled face softened at the thought of Jasper Dysart. He was a dear old man, but she hadn't seen him in months because he lived in Spain most of the year, having found the hot climate eased his arthritic joints.

Dixie had met Jasper the previous summer. She had been walking down the street when a thuggish bunch of youths had carelessly pushed

him aside when he didn't get out of their way
fast enough. Jasper had fallen and cut his head.
Dixie had taken him to the nearest hospital. Afterwards, she had treated him to tea and buns in
the cafeteria, because he had looked so poor and
forlorn in his ancient tweeds and shabby old
overcoat.

They had been firm friends from that moment
on. She hadn't once suspected that Jasper might
be anything other than he appeared: an elderly
academic living on a restricted income. So she
had been quite honest about being unemployed,
sharing her despair at not even being able to get
as far as an interview for a clerical job. She had
also told him how horribly guilty she felt about
being dependent on her older sister Petra's gen-
erosity.

They had arranged to meet up again, and
Jasper had escorted Dixie to his favourite sec-
ondhand bookshop, where they had both
promptly lost all track of time browsing through
the shelves. The following weekend she had returned the favour by taking him to a library sale,
where he had contrived to buy a very tattered
copy of an out-of-print tome on butterflies that
he had been trying to find for years.

And then quite casually Jasper had announced
that he had fixed her up with an interview at the
Valverde Mercantile Bank. 'I put in a word for

you with my godson,' he had informed her cheerfully. 'He was very happy to help.'

She hadn't had a clue that Jasper's godson was
the chief executive. And she had been utterly appalled to be confronted by César Valverde that
first day, and coldly interrogated about exactly
how she had met his godfather. He had made
little attempt to conceal his suspicions about her
motives in fostering such a friendship with an
elderly man, and had coolly enjoyed informing
her that Jasper would be returning to his home
in Spain at the end of September. Dixie had
found that encounter deeply humiliating.

'César always had a head for figures...very
clever chap with that sort of stuff,' Jasper had
conceded vaguely when Dixie had later gently
taxed him with his failure to tell her that his godson *ran* Valverde Mercantile and was, in fact, a
super-rich and very powerful legend of thrusting
success in the financial world. 'It's in his blood.'

Jasper was a genius at understatement. The
Valverdes had been in banking for generations.
César was the last of the dynasty, and reputedly
the most brilliant. He also had very high expectations of his staff. All Dixie's colleagues had a
university degree in financial management, eco-
nomics or languages, and thrived on the cracking
pace of a high-powered mercantile bank with an

international list of hugely important clients and companies.

Dixie knew that she was a fish out of water at Valverde Mercantile, only fit, it sometimes seemed, to run messages, ensure the coffee machines stayed filled and perform the most humble of tasks. She worked really hard at keeping busy, but the kind of lowly work she did rarely produced results that other people could appreciate.

And Bruce Gregory's announcement had thoroughly shaken Dixie. The threat of a face-to-face meeting with César Valverde kept her stomach churning throughout the day. What had she done? What had she *not* done? Well, if she had made some awful mistake or oversight, she would have to grovel on her knees and promise to do better in the future; she had no choice.

Right now, the only thing keeping Dixie going through exhaustion was the knowledge that she had a steady salary coming in as well as what she earned working as a waitress several nights a week. That long talk she had had with the helpful lady at the Citizens' Advice Bureau had suggested that as long as she could prove an honest intent to pay back those creditors in instalments, her offer to do so should be acceptable, and would hopefully protect her from the threat of legal proceedings.

And, in the meantime, there was always the hope that her sister Petra would phone to say that she was back in funds again and able to send the money to clear her debts. Petra had always had terrific earning power as a model, Dixie reminded herself bracingly. All she herself was really doing was holding the fort until her sister could pick up the financial slack. Petra *had* been upset when Dixie called her to tell her about the bills she had neglected to pay before she flew out to Los Angeles in the hope of starting an acting career.

In the cloakroom, minutes to go before the encounter, Dixie freshened up and morosely surveyed her reflection. Plain and wholesome, that was her. The loose beige top and long grey cotton skirt at least concealed the worst of her deficiencies, she told herself in consolation. But as always it seemed particularly cruel to Dixie that she should have been endowed with hatefully large breasts and generous hips but only a height of five feet two inches.

As often happened at times of particular stress, Dixie drifted off into her own thoughts. Was it any wonder that Scott saw her as a good sport and a mate, rather than a possible girlfriend? Scott Lewis, handsome, extrovert and the love of Dixie's life. Momentarily, self-pity filled her to overflowing. And then she scolded herself for being so foolish. Hadn't she always known she didn't have a hope of attracting Scott?

She had met Scott at one of her sister's parties. Having just moved into a new apartment, he'd been giving a comic description of his less than successful efforts to get organised on the domestic front. His frank admission that his mother had spoilt him rotten had impressed Dixie, and before she had even thought about what she was doing she had found herself offering to come round and give him a hand…

When Dixie presented herself for her appointment, César Valverde's secretary, a svelte brunette in her thirties, gave her a pained look. 'It might have been a good idea to be on time, Dixie.'

'But I am on time.' Dixie checked her watch and then her face fell. Once again time had run on without her.

'You're ten minutes late.' The other woman didn't wince but she might as well have done.

Sick with apprehension, Dixie knocked on the door of her lofty employer's office and walked in, a band of tension tightening round her head, her mouth bone-dry and her palms damp.

César Valverde spun lithely round from the wall of glass which overlooked the City skyline and studied her. 'You're late,' he delivered icily.

'I'm really sorry...I just don't know where the time went.' Dixie studied the deep-pile carpet, wishing it would open up and swallow her and disgorge her only when the interview was safely over.

'That is not an acceptable excuse.'

'That's why I apologised,' Dixie pointed out in a very small voice without looking up.

There was really no need to look up. In her mind's eye she could still see César Valverde standing there, as formidable and unfeeling as a hitman. And close to him she always felt murderously awkward, not to mention all hot and bothered. Yet he was physically quite beautiful, a little voice pointed out absently inside her head.

He had the lean dark face of a fallen angel, blessed with such perfect bone structure that at first glance he knocked women flat with his spectacular sleek Mediterranean looks. Hair thick and glossy as ebony. Eyes the same colour as dark bitter chocolate, which blazed into the strangest silver in strong light. Mouth mobile, wide and sensual. A sensationally attractive male animal, but at second glance he had always chilled Dixie to the marrow.

Those stunning eyes were hard and cold, that shapely mouth rarely smiled, except at someone else's misfortune, and those sculpted cheekbones stamped his features with a quality of merciless unemotional detachment which intimidated. He might radiate raw sexuality like a forcefield, but Dixie still prided herself on being the only woman in the whole building who was repulsed by César Valverde. The guy could give a freezer pneumonia just by arching one satiric brow.

Belatedly conscious of the dragging silence, Dixie emerged from her own reflections and glanced nervously up. Her pupils dilated, her heartbeat quickening as she stared. A decided frown on his striking dark features, César Valverde was strolling in a soundless circle round her, his piercing gaze intent on her now shrinking figure.

'What's wrong?' she breathed, thoroughly disconcerted by his behaviour and the intensity of his scrutiny.

'*Dio mio…*what's *right*?' His frown deepened as her slight shoulders drooped. 'Straighten up… don't slouch like that,' he told her.

Flushing, Dixie did as she was told. She was relieved when he positioned himself against the edge of his immaculately tidy glass desk.

'Do you recall the terms of the employment contract you signed before you started work here?'

Dixie thought about that and then guiltily shook her head. She had had to fill in and sign an avalanche of papers at speed that first day.

'You didn't bother to study the contract,' César gathered with a curled lip.

'I was desperate for a job...I would have signed anything.'

'But if you'd read your contract, you would have known that getting into debt is grounds for instant dismissal.'

That unexpected revelation struck Dixie like a sudden blow. She stared at him in horror, soft full lips falling apart, what colour there was in her cheeks slowly, painfully draining away. César studied her the way a shark studies wounded prey before moving in for the kill. In silence he extended a computer printout.

With an unsteady hand, Dixie grasped at the sheet. Her heart felt as if it was thumping at the foot of her throat, making it impossible for her to breathe. The same names and figures which already haunted her every waking hour swam before her eyes and her tummy flipped in shock.

'Security turned that up this morning. Regular financial checks are made on all staff,' César informed her smoothly.

'You're sacking me,' Dixie assumed sickly, swaying slightly.

Striding forward, César reached for a chair and planted it beside her. 'Sit down, Miss Robinson.'

Dixie fumbled blindly down into the chair before her knees gave way beneath her. She was waiting for him to ask how such a junior employee could possibly have amassed debts amounting to such a staggering total. Indeed, in that instant of overwhelming shock and embarrassment, she was actually eager to explain how, through a series of awful misunderstandings and mishaps, such a situation had developed through no real fault of her own.

'I have not the slightest interest in hearing a sob story,' César Valverde delivered deflatingly as he lounged back against his desk again, his impossibly tall, lean and powerful length taking up a formidably relaxed pose.

'But I *want* to explain—'

'There is no need for you to explain anything. Debts of that nature are self-explanatory. You have a taste for living above your means and you like to party—'

Cringing at the knowledge that he knew about those shameful debts in her name, and her equally shameful inability to settle them, Dixie broke back into speech. '*No*, Mr Valverde. I—'

'If you interrupt me again, I won't offer you my assistance,' César Valverde interposed with icy bite.

Struggling to understand that assurance, Dixie tipped back her wildly curly head and gaped at him. '*Assistance?*' she stressed blankly.

'I'm prepared to offer you another form of employment.'

In complete confusion, Dixie blinked.

'But if you take on the role, it will entail a great deal of hard work and effort on your part.'

Sinking ever deeper into bewilderment, but ready to snatch at any prospect of continuing employment like a drowning swimmer snatches at a branch, Dixie nodded eagerly. 'I'm not afraid of hard work, Mr Valverde.'

Obviously he was talking about demoting her. Where did you go from office junior? Dixie wondered frantically. Scrubbing the floors in the canteen kitchen?

César sent her a gleaming glance. 'You're really not in a position to turn my offer down.'

'I know,' Dixie acknowledged with total humility, suddenly starting to squirm at the reality of how much she had always disliked him. Evidently she had completely misjudged César Valverde's character. Even though he had a legitimate excuse to sack her, he seemed to be willing to give her another chance. And if that meant scrubbing the canteen kitchen floor, she ought to say thank you from the bottom of her heart and get on with it.

'Jasper hasn't been well.'

The switch in subject disconcerted Dixie. Her strained face shadowed. 'By what he's said in his letters he still hasn't quite got over that chest trouble he had in the spring.'

César looked grim. 'His heart is weak.'

Dixie's eyes prickled. That news was too much on top of all her other worries. Her stinging eyes overflowed and she dug into the pocket of her skirt to find a tissue. But the horrible news about Jasper did make sudden sense of César Valverde's uncharacteristic tolerance, and his apparent willingness to allow her to remain in his employment by fixing her up with another job. He might not approve of her, or of her friendship with Jasper Dysart, but clearly he respected his godfather's fondness for her. Presumably that was why he wasn't going to kick her when she was already down.

'At his age, Jasper can't hope to go on for ever,' César gritted, his unease with her emotional breakdown blatant and icily reproving.

Fighting to compose herself, Dixie blew her nose and sucked in a deep, steadying breath. 'Will he be coming over to London this summer?'

'I shouldn't think so.'

Then she would never see Jasper again, she registered on a powerful tide of pain and regret. The struggle to stay abreast of the debts Petra had left behind made a trip to Spain as out of reach as a trip to the moon.

'It's time we got down to business,' César drawled with perceptible impatience. 'I need a favour, and in return for that favour I'm prepared to settle your debts.'

'Settle my debts...what favour?' Dixie echoed, all at sea as to what he could possibly be talking about and stunned by the idea of him offering to pay off those appalling bills. A favour? What sort of favour? How could her staying employed in any capacity within the Valverde Mercantile Bank be any kind of a favour to César Valverde?

César moved restively away from the desk and strode over to the window, the clear light of early summer glittering over his luxuriant hair and hard, classic profile. 'In all probability, Jasper doesn't have long to live,' he spelt out harshly. 'His dearest wish has always been that I should marry. At this present time I have no intention of fulfilling that wish, but I would very much like to please him with a harmless fiction.'

A harmless fiction? Dixie's bemusement increased as she strained to grasp his meaning.

'And that is where you come in,' César informed her drily. 'Jasper likes you. He's very shy with your sex, and as a result he only warms to a certain type of woman. *Your* type. Jasper would be overjoyed if I announced that we had got engaged.'

'We…?' Dixie whispered weakly, certain she had missed a connecting link somewhere in that speech and beginning to stand up, as if by rising from the chair she might comprehend something that she couldn't follow while still sitting.

César wheeled round, a forbidding cast to his lean features. 'Your job would be to pretend that you're engaged to me. It would be a private arrangement between us. You would play the role solely for Jasper's benefit in Spain.'

A curious whirring sound reverberated in Dixie's eardrums. Her lungs seemed suddenly empty of oxygen. Disbelief paralysing her, she gazed wide-eyed across the room at César Valverde. 'You can't be serious… *Me*,' she stressed helplessly, 'pretend to be engaged to…to *you*?'

'Jasper will be convinced. People are always keen to believe what they *want* to believe,' César asserted with rich cynicism.

As yet uncertain that this weird conversation was actually taking place, Dixie moved her head in a negative motion. 'But nobody would believe *that*…that you and I…' A betraying tide of colour slowly washed up her throat into her cheeks. 'I mean, it's just so *un*believable!'

'That's where your upcoming hard work and effort will pay off.' Once again César studied her with that curious considering frown he had worn earlier. 'I intend to make this charade as credible as possible. Jasper may be naive, but he's no fool. Only when I've finished transforming you into a slimline, elegant Dixie Mark Two will Jasper bc truly convinced.'

It crossed Dixie's mind that César Valverde had been at the booze. A slimline Dixie Mark Two? She snatched in a short, sustaining breath. 'Mr Valverde, I—'

'Yes, I expect you're very grateful,' César dismissed arrogantly, a scornful light in his brilliant dark eyes as he surveyed her. 'In fact I imagine you can hardly credit your good luck—'

'My good luck?' Dixie broke in shakily, wondering how any male so famed for his perception could be so wildly off course when it came to reading her reactions.

'An image makeover, a new wardrobe, all your debts paid *and* an all-expenses-paid trip to Spain?' César enumerated with cool exactitude. 'It's more than good luck…from where you're standing now, it's the equivalent of striking oil in the desert wastes! And you don't deserve it. Believe me, if I had an alternative choice of fiancée available you'd have been fired first thing this morning!'

'I was the *only* choice, wasn't I?' Dixie gathered in a wobbly voice. '*Your* type,' he had said minutes ago, the only woman liked by Jasper that

César Valverde knew. A slimline Dixie Mark Two? How dared he get as personal as that? Didn't he even appreciate that she had feelings that could be hurt? But then why should he care, standing there all lean and fit and perfect, probably never having had to watch his appetite once in his entire spoilt rotten life!

'That's irrelevant. By the way, I want this arrangement of ours to stay under wraps.' César scanned her with threatening dark eyes. 'Do you understand the concept of keeping a secret, Dixie?'

Locked to those spectacular dark eyes, Dixie felt oddly dizzy and out of breath. 'A secret?'

'It's quite simple. If you open your mouth to another living soul about this deal, I'll bury you,' César Valverde murmured with chilling bite.

Dixie blenched. 'That's not very funny.'

'It wasn't meant to be. It was a warning. And you've been in here long enough. As soon as you walk out of this office, you can clear your desk and go home. I'll be in touch this evening so that we can work out the finer details.'

Dixie lifted her chin, her rarely roused temper rising at the arrogance with which he simply assumed that she would do whatever he told her to do, no matter how immoral or unpleasant it might be. 'Whatever decision I make, I can now consider myself sacked...isn't that right?'

'Wow, quick on the uptake,' César derided smoothly. 'Too dumb to safely operate anything with a plug attached, but reads Nietzsche and Plato in her spare time. According to Jasper, you have a remarkable brain. And yet you never do anything with it. You certainly never dreamt of bringing it into work with you—'

Her lashes fluttered over huge violet eyes. 'I beg your—?'

'But then that's because you're a lazy, disorganised lump, who contrives to hide behind the front of being a brick short of the full load! Only around me you won't get away with that kind of nonsense!'

Disbelief roared through Dixie as she reeled from the full impact of that derisive attack, even though on another level she longed to question him about Jasper having said that she had a remarkable brain. However, anger abruptly overpowered that brief spark of surprised pleasure and curiosity. 'If I can consider myself sacked, then I'm free to tell you exactly what I think of you too!'

César gave her a wolfish half-smile of encouragement. 'I'm enjoying this. The office doormat suddenly discovers backbone. Make my day... Only be warned—I will respond in kind.'

Teeth almost chattering with the force of her disturbed emotions, Dixie drew herself up to her full unimpressive height and hissed, 'You have to be the most unscrupulous, selfish human being I have ever met! Doesn't it even occur to you that I might have some moral objection to cruelly deceiving a sweet old man, who deserves better from a male he loves like a son?'

'You're right. That thought didn't occur to me,' César confessed, without a shade of discomfiture or remorse. 'Considering that you're currently on the brink of being taken to court for obtaining goods and services by fraudulent deception, I'm not remotely impressed by the sound of your moral scruples!'

Dixie shrank and turned white. 'Taken to c-court?' she stammered, aghast, her eyes nailed to him in the hope that she had somehow misunderstood.

CHAPTER TWO

'*DIO mio...*' César raised a winging ebony brow to challenge Dixie's stricken expression. 'Didn't you read that printout I gave you either? The interior designer, Leticia Zane, has instigated proceedings. Did you expect her to be sympathetic towards a client who took advantage of her services without the slightest hope of being able to pay for them?'

Numbly, Dixie shook her pounding head, her stomach curdling. 'But I haven't got any more money to give Miss Zane...I've already offered instalments.'

César Valverde shifted a broad shoulder in an unfeeling shrug. 'The lady may well have decided to make a public spectacle of you to deter other clients who are reluctant to settle up. You're a good choice—'

'A good choice?' Dixie parroted, scarcely believing her ears.

'You don't have socially prominent friends likely to take offence on your behalf and damage her business prospects.'

'But...but a court prosecution.' Dixie squeezed out those words, breathless with horror, utterly appalled by what he was spelling out to her. Her own naivety hit her hard. She stared down at the printout, belatedly reading the small type beneath the debt to Leticia Zane's firm. 'Prosecution pending', it said. Her blood ran cold with fear and incredulity. The interior designer knew very well that all the work on her sister's apartment had been done at Petra's behest. Dixie had merely been the mouthpiece who'd passed on the instructions.

'Delusions of grandeur have a price, like everything else,' César Valverde sighed.

'I can't think straight,' Dixie mumbled sickly.

'Sharpen up. I haven't got all day to wait for an answer that is already staring you in the face,' César breathed with callous cool.

Dixie gave him a speaking glance from tear-filled eyes and fumbled with the crushed tissue still clutched between her shaking fingers. 'I just couldn't deceive Jasper like that, Mr Valverde. I couldn't live with lying to him. It would be absolutely wrong!'

'You're being selfish and shortsighted,' César drawled crushingly, dealing her a look of hostile reproach. 'Getting engaged to you is the one thing that I can do to make Jasper happy. What right have you to say that it would be wrong or immoral?'

'Lies are always wrong!' Dixie sobbed helplessly, and turned away from him in embarrassment.

'Jasper won't ever know it was a lie. He'll be delighted. I plan to leave you with him in Spain for a few weeks...assuming he's well enough for me to leave, even temporarily,' César adjusted flatly.

'I couldn't...I just *couldn't*!' Dixie gasped strickenly, already plotting a weaving path towards the door, barely able to see through her falling tears but determined not to be swayed by his specious arguments. 'And it's wicked of you to call me selfish. How can you *do* that?'

'For Jasper's sake...easily. I'll call on you tonight to get your final answer. I think you'll have seen sense by then.'

Dixie hauled open the door with a trembling hand and shot him an angry, accusing glance. 'Go to hell!' she launched thickly as she walked out.

Only as she shut the door behind her did she notice the little clutch of staff standing with dropped jaws further down the corridor.

'And you OK, Dixie?' Bruce Gregory enquired kindly.

One of the directors put his arm round her in a very paternal way to walk her away. 'We'll get you sorted out with a job some place else.'

'Not in a bank,' someone whispered ruefully.

'Ever thought of cooking for a living?' another voice asked brightly. 'You're a great cook.'

'A restaurant kitchen could be very stressful, though.'

'And I drop things,' Dixie muttered, a sense of being a total failure creeping over her.

'Imagine you telling César to go to hell!' the director remarked bracingly.

'But he'll never let Personnel give her a decent reference now,' Bruce groaned as the older man slotted her into a seat in the office she shared with a couple of the secretaries. Just about everybody on the whole floor seemed to crowd around her then.

'He tried to blackmail me,' Dixie mumbled sickly.

'Say that again…' someone breathed.

Dixie reddened, and then turned very pale with fright at what she had almost revealed in her distress and buttoned her mouth. 'Don't mind me…I don't know what I'm s-saying,' she stammered fearfully.

And she registered then that her brain was in a state of complete flux. What César Valverde had suggested already seemed completely unreal, a figment of her own fevered imagination. A fake engagement to please Jasper? A fantasy slimline Dixie Mark Two, united even in pretence with César's icy sophistication? Did blue moons come up in pairs?

'I don't know what we're going to do for a laugh around here now,' someone lamented.

'You'll have to get your goldfish out of the fountain...wasn't the ideal environment for them anyway. César raised Cain when he saw you out there feeding them,' Bruce reminded her ruefully.

'There's only one now, and I don't even have an aquarium!' Dixie sobbed, because it felt like absolutely the last straw. To take her goldfish out of the fountain below César Valverde's office and never, ever come back into the building? Suddenly she felt completely bereft and cut adrift.

Across the room, her desk was being cleared for her. One carrier bag grew into three as books, knitting, fish food and sundry items were removed from the crammed drawers. Tissues were supplied and a glass of water was pressed on her.

'We're all going to really miss you, Dixie...so we had a bit of a whip round.' She was mortified when a large fat envelope was thrust by Bruce into her shoulder bag. She realised then that everyone had known even before she did that she was getting the sack, and had been waiting to comfort her.

'I'll give you a lift home with your bags,' Bruce volunteered.

The chipped china jardinière was filched from beneath the dying cactus on her desk, and the goldfish she had found abandoned at the bus stop in a plastic bag removed with some difficulty from the fountain and temporarily rehoused.

'I just can't get over how kind everyone's been,' Dixie confided as she climbed into Bruce's car in the basement car park.

She clutched the planter with careful hands, gazing down at the single handsome goldfish she had secretly christened, César. He had eaten his original companion, and even the one she'd actually bought for him, fearing that he would be lonely. César the fish was up near the surface, patrolling with fast flicks of his tail. Dixie gave him a loving and abstracted smile.

'César can be a real bastard. But the guy's a complete genius. You can't expect him to be human too. Try not to think about it. Go round and do Scott's washing...or whatever,' Bruce advised, striving to be upbeat. 'That always seems to give you a lift.'

Yes, it did, she acknowledged ruefully, only this evening she would be waiting tables. But doing anything for Scott gave her the feeling that she had some small personal stake in his busy life. And in the right mood, if Scott didn't have a hot date or wasn't eating out, he might suggest that she cooked some supper and stayed to eat with him. She *lived* for those infrequent invitations.

'You were in with César a very long time,' Bruce commented abruptly.

'We talked a little about Jasper.'

'Dixie…why did you say César tried to blackmail you?'

'I must've been trying to make a silly joke…'

Bruce sent her scared face a covert appraisal. 'He never did approve of your friendship with the old man. Can't think why.'

As soon as Bruce had carried her bags upstairs for her, he left to speed back to the office, long hours being a feature of his highly paid employment. Dixie unlocked the door of her bedsit. She transferred César the fish into a large glass mixing bowl and fed him, setting him next to the window in the hope that a view of the pigeons on the roof opposite would keep him entertained.

Locking up again, she went down the street to call in on a neighbour she often babysat for at weekends. In return the older woman kept her Jack Russell dog, Spike, during the day.

She took Spike for a quick walk in the park, and then nervously carried him back up to her bedsit for the night. She wasn't allowed to keep pets, but she had never had any bother sneaking Spike in after it got dark. Now that the light nights had arrived, she was really scared that she would be seen.

How on earth had her life got into such a terrible, frightening mess? she asked herself in a daze as she watched Spike wolf down his dinner. The future had looked so promising when she had first come up to London to share Petra's spacious apartment, certainly a lot brighter than it had seemed for many years beforehand…

Dixie's mother had died when she was five and her father had remarried the following year. It was hard to recall even now that Petra wasn't really her true sister but actually her *step*sister— the daughter of her father's second wife, Muriel. Already a teenager, Petra had had little interest in a child seven years younger, but Dixie had always longed for a big sister and had adored blonde and beautiful Petra. At seventeen, Petra had left home on her first modelling assignment.

A year later, Dixie's father had died of a heart attack, and the year after that Muriel had shown the first symptoms of what was to prove to be a long, debilitating terminal illness. Dixie had never managed to pass any exams because she had been forced to miss so much school. Whenever Muriel's health had been particularly bad, Dixie had had to stay at home to see to her needs. She had left school at sixteen.

Over the following four years, Petra had sent money home regularly but the demands of a career which took her all over the world had made it impossible for her to visit much. A year ago, Muriel Robinson had passed away, and Dixie had more or less invited herself up to London to stay with Petra. Used to living alone, Petra had understandably not been too keen on the arrangement at first, but had soon appreciated that Dixie could look after her apartment when she herself was abroad.

For her own convenience, Petra had opened a household account in both their names, and paid in sufficient money to cover her bills, so that Dixie could easily pay them for her. And when, soon afterwards, Dixie had started work at Valverde Mercantile, she had had her entire salary paid into the same account.

Dixie had frequently ordered expensive food and alcohol for Petra's lavish parties. In the same way she had dealt with Leticia Zane, after the interior designer's initial meeting with Petra, ensuring that all the costly redecoration was done in exactly the way her sister wished.

And then, about three months ago, Petra had suddenly announced that she was leaving the UK. Giving up the lease on her apartment, she had packed her bags and flown to Los Angeles. Dixie had moved into the bedsit. But within weeks the demands for payment had begun rolling in from her sister's creditors. Dixie had discovered that the joint account was not only empty of her own savings but also overdrawn. Only after the deputy bank manager had patiently explained it to her had Dixie understood that she herself could be held liable for Petra's unpaid bills.

She had immediately phoned her sister. After admitting that she was broke, but promising to help as soon as she could, Petra had rather drily reminded Dixie of all the money she had generously sent over the years that Dixie had been nursing her mother, Muriel. And Dixie had felt really guilty, because tough as those years had been they would have been intolerable without Petra's financial assistance.

But the next time Dixie had phoned that same number she had been told that Petra had moved on without leaving a forwarding address. That had been two months ago, and since then she hadn't heard a word from her sister.

The awful fear that Petra had not the slightest intention of getting in touch again, or of trying to satisfy her creditors, was now beginning to haunt Dixie. She felt so disloyal, thinking about Petra that way. Yet in her heart of hearts she was facing up to the harsh fact that her glamorous stepsister invariably put her own needs first.

And Dixie was terrified of being taken to court and appalled by the reality that she had no way of settling those dreadful bills. That was so unfair to the creditors concerned, and César Valverde *had* offered to pay them…

'Can I just run over this again?' Dixie asked the table of customers anxiously. 'That's one cheese-burger with pickles, one without dressing, a dou-ble—'

'How many times do we have to go over this?' one of the teenagers groaned. 'A double ham-burger *with* pickles, a single cheeseburger *with-out*…'

Pink with embarrassment, Dixie hurried to amend her notebook as the girl ran through the entire order again. Beneath the jaundiced eye of the manager, Dixie thrust the order over the counter.

'Get those tables cleared,' he urged impa-tiently.

Scurrying over to her section of the busy café, Dixie began to load up a tray. She was so tired that she could feel her knees wobbling whenever she stood still. Wiping her damp brow with the back of her hand, she lifted the heavily laden tray. As she straightened, she could not help but focus on the tall, dark male blocking her view of the rest of the cafe. Dixie froze in shock and dismay.

César Valverde stood six feet away, emanating the kind of lacerating cool which intimidated. Brilliant dark eyes entrapped her evasive ones. As he lifted one ebony brow at her frazzled appearance and coffee-stained overall, Dixie simply wanted to curl up and die. Oh, dear heaven, how had he found out where she worked? And what did he want now, for heaven's sake?

But then had she really believed that César Valverde would take no for an answer? He wasn't accustomed to negative responses. His naturally aggressive temperament geared him to persist and demand in the face of refusal, she reminded herself. A workaholic, he thrived under pressure and lived for challenge. When César Valverde set himself a goal, he went all out to get it. She should feel sorry for him, she told herself. He really didn't know any other way to behave.

An exasperated male voice demanded, 'Where's our food?'

'It's coming…it's coming!' Dixie promised frantically, rudely dredged from her reverie. She fled without looking where she was going, as to look would have brought César Valverde back into focus again.

A shopping bag protruding from beneath a table was her undoing. Catching her foot, Dixie tipped forward, and the tray shot clean out of her perspiring hold. Eyes wide with horror, she watched pieces of food, coffee dregs, crumpled napkins, plates and cups go flying up in the air and fall in all directions. The noise of smashing china was equalled if not surpassed by the shaken exclamations of customers lurching from their seats in an effort to escape the aerial bombardment.

A deathly silence fell in the aftermath. Feverishly muttering incoherent apologies, Dixie bent down to scoop up the tray. The manager removed it from her trembling hands and hissed in her ear, 'You had your final warning yesterday. You're fired!'

Only yesterday, three entire meals complete with accompanying drinks had landed on the floor, because in an effort to speed up Dixie had overloaded a tray and then stumbled. Tears of mortification and defeat stinging her eyes, Dixie scuttled into the back of the café. Ripping off the overall, she reached for her cardigan and bag.

When she emerged again, the manager stuffed a couple of notes into her hand. 'You're just not cut out for waitressing,' he said ruefully.

A long, low and expensive sports car hugged the pavement outside the café. The driver's window whirred down. César surveyed Dixie with an enquiring brow.

'It's your fault I dropped that tray...you spooked me!' Dixie condemned unevenly.

'If you hadn't been so busy trying to ignore me it wouldn't have happened.'

'You are so smug and patronising. I hate you!' Dixie gasped truthfully, studying his staggeringly handsome dark features with unconcealed loathing. 'You always think you're right about everything!'

'I usually am,' César pointed out, without skipping a beat.

'Not about deceiving Jasper...so go away and leave me alone!'

Walking on past, Dixie struggled to swallow the aching thickness of tears in her throat. The car purred in her wake but Dixie was oblivious. In the space of one ghastly day a security that had at best been tenuous had come crashing down round her ears. Jasper was dying, she thought wretchedly, and she was going to end up being prosecuted like a criminal.

'Get in the car, Dixie!'

Having totally forgotten about César Valverde while she pondered her woes, Dixie nearly died of fright. She glanced round and saw the flash car only feet away. Sticking her nose in the air, she prepared to cross the road to the bus stop.

'Get...in...the car,' César framed as he climbed out, six foot three inches of towering bully.

'I don't have to do what you tell me any more!' Dixie flung chokily.

A policeman crossed the road. 'Is there some problem here?'

'Yes, this man won't leave me alone!' Dixie complained.

'I saw you kerb-crawling,' the policeman informed César thinly. 'Are you aware that kerb-crawling is an offence?'

'This woman works for me, Officer,' César drawled icily.

'Not any more, I don't!' Dixie protested. 'Why won't you just leave me alone?'

'I don't like the sound of this, sir.' The policeman appraised the opulent car and then the cut of César's fabulous dark grey suit with deeply suspicious eyes.

'Look, that's my bus coming!' Dixie suddenly gasped.

'Settle the misunderstanding, Dixie,' César commanded in a tone of icy warning.

'What misunderstanding?' she enquired in honest bewilderment.

'This gentleman was kerb-crawling and employing threatening behaviour. I think we should all go back to the station and sort this out,' the policeman informed her as he radioed in the registration of César's car.

César looked at Dixie. Eyes like black ice daggers dug into her. It was like being hauled off her feet and dropped from a height. She blinked, and then warm colour flooded her drawn cheeks. 'Oh...you actually think...my goodness, are you kidding?' she pressed in a strangled voice. 'He would never bother *me* like that...I mean, he would never even *look* at me like that!'

'Then what was this gentleman doing?' the policeman asked wearily.

'He was offering me a lift home...and we had a slight difference of opinion,' Dixie mumbled, not looking at either man in her mortification. This policeman had *genuinely* suspected that César Valverde had been kerb-crawling with an intent to...?

'And now she's going to get in my car and be sensible,' César completed stonily.

Dixie slunk round the sports car and climbed in. 'It's not my fault that policeman thought you might've been making improper suggestions,' she muttered in hot-faced embarrassment.

'Oh, don't worry about that. That *wasn't* what he was thinking. He thought I might be your pimp,' César gritted not very levelly, half under his breath, his accented drawl alive with speaking undertones of raw incredulity.

Dixie nestled into the gloriously comfortable bucket seat and decided that silence was the better part of valour. Flash car, flash suit. In this particular area César probably had looked suspicious.

'How *dare* you embarrass me like that?'

'I'm sorry, but you were annoying me,' she mumbled wearily.

'*I*...was annoying...*you*?'

He seemed to find that very difficult to understand. But then an enormous amount of bootlicking went on in César Valverde's vicinity, Dixie reflected, struggling to smother a yawn.

People shouldn't worship idols, but they did. Expose the average human being to César's intellectual brilliance, immense wealth and enormous power and influence, and they generally behaved in all sorts of undignified ways. They toadied, they talked a load of rubbish in an effort to impress, and went to ridiculous lengths to please and be remembered by him.

As for the women—that constant procession of gorgeous females who paraded through his life, Dixie reflected sleepily. Well, he had the concentration span of a toddler, always on the look-out for a new and better toy. And he invariably had a replacement lined up before he ditched her predecessor. But he was never available during working hours, and those women who tried to breach that boundary lasted the least time. Possessive behaviour was a surefire way to make César stray.

César shook her awake outside the building where she lived. 'As a rule, women do not fall asleep in my company.'

'I don't fancy you,' Dixie mumbled, barely half awake, and then aghast at the sound of what she had just said.

'Then you won't develop any ambitious ideas while we're in Spain, will you?'

'I'm not going to Spain.'

'Then you can send Jasper cute ''glad you're not here'' postcards from prison.'

Dixie sat up, full wakefulness now established, and turned aghast eyes on him.

César gave her a faint smile. 'It's your first offence, but who knows? Women often get weightier sentences than men when they transgress.'

Her tummy tying itself into petrified knots, Dixie whispered shakily. 'Maybe we should talk this over.'

'I think we ought to,' César agreed smoothly. 'A female who said she was your landlady cut up rough when I knocked on the door of your bedsit earlier and a dog started barking. She came upstairs to investigate.'

Dixie sat bolt upright, horror now etched on her face. 'Oh, no, she heard Spike and now she knows he's there!'

César released an extravagant sigh. 'And pets aren't allowed. I gather it's going to be a question of moving out or getting rid of the dog.'

Dixie shook her head in anguished disbelief. This was truly the very worst day of her entire life. 'Why did you have to knock on the door? You must've frightened Spike! He's usually as quiet as a mouse.'

'I think Spain's beckoning,' César remarked lazily. 'You have one very angry landlady waiting to pounce.'

'*Oh, no…*' Dixie groaned.

'Life could be so different,' César drawled smoothly. 'All those debts settled…no nasty hanging judge to face in court…relaxing trip to Spain…Jasper happy as a sandboy and the comforting knowledge that you are responsible for giving him the best news he's ever heard. *Wrong?* I don't think so. I don't think anything that could give Jasper pleasure at this trying stage of his life could possibly be wrong.'

Hanging on every specious word, Dixie watched him with a kind of eerie fascination. He was so damnably clever, so shockingly good at timing his verbal assaults. Here she was, her whole life in ruins and on the very brink of being thrown out on the street because she couldn't possibly give up Spike, and a living, breathing version of the devil was holding out temptation without shame.

'I couldn't…'

'You could,' César contradicted softly. 'You could do it for Jasper.'

Dixie's soft full mouth wobbled as she thought of Jasper dying and never, ever seeing him again. Her eyes began to prickle and she sniffed.

'You can pack right now. It's *that* simple,' César stressed in the same low-pitched deep, dark tone.

He sounded mesmeric. Dixie couldn't peel her wet eyes from him either. In the dusk light, his bronzed features were half in shadow, dark eyes glimmering silver beneath the sort of long, incredibly luxuriant black lashes that would drive any sane woman blessed with less to despair.

'My dog, Spike…' she muttered uncertainly, so very, very tired it was becoming an effort even to string words together, her mind a confused sea of incomplete thoughts and fears.

'Spike can come too. One of my staff will pick up the rest of your possessions tomorrow. You won't have anything to do,' César asserted gently.

At that moment, the concept of not having anything to do impressed Dixie like the offer of manna from heaven. 'I...I—'

César slid out of the driver's seat, strolled round the bonnet and opened the door beside her. 'Come on,' he urged.

And Dixie found herself doing as she was told, all the fight drained out of her. 'A harmless fiction', César had called it. A pretend engagement to make Jasper's last days happy. And it *would* make Jasper happy. She knew how much Jasper longed to see César on the road to creating the family circle that Jasper had never managed to create for himself. Maybe lying wasn't always wrong...

Her landlady emerged from her small flat on the ground floor. As she broke into angry, accusing speech, César settled a wad of banknotes into her hand. 'Miss Robinson will be moving out. I hope this takes care of her notice.'

A phone was ringing somewhere horribly close to Dixie's ears. Struggling to cling to sleep, she sighed with relief when the shrill buzz stopped, but her eyes slowly opened on the dawning realisation that she didn't have a phone in her bedsit.

Her brain in a fog, Dixie surveyed her unfamiliar surroundings. For a moment she couldn't even remember where she was. Then her attention fell on the suitcase lying open with miscellaneous garments tumbling untidily out of it. And whoosh, everything came back in a rush; she was in César Valverde's London home.

The phone by the bed started ringing again. This time Dixie reached for the receiver. 'Hello?' she said nervously.

'Rise and shine, Dixie.' César Valverde's rich, dark drawl jerked her bolt upright in the bed. 'It's half-six and I want you in the gym by eight, dressed appropriately and fully awake.'

'The gym?' Dixie was aghast at the news that she was expected to be up before seven in the morning, particularly on a Saturday. Even Spike was still asleep in his basket. He was as fond of having a lie-in as his owner.

'I've engaged a fitness instructor to put you through your paces,' César completed drily, and rang off.

A fitness instructor? Dixie stared into space with wide eyes, picturing some giant, suntanned musclebound male standing over her like a bullying sergeant-major, bawling instructions liberally splattered with abuse. She shrank. Maybe the instructor would be nice and break her in gently. She tried to imagine César hiring someone nice. Hope dwindled fast. The fitness instructor would be tough and pitiless. César was, after all, the male who had called her a lazy lump.

Scrambling out of bed, Dixie roused Spike and left the bedroom. A short corridor beyond led out to a small enclosed courtyard.

On her arrival the night before, Dixie had been handed over to César's butler, Fisher, like a unwelcome parcel. The comfortable *en suite* bedroom she had been assigned on the ground floor was former staff accommodation. Dixie had understood the distinction being made. She was not going to be treated like an honoured guest in César Valverde's palatial Georgian mansion.

Having attended to Spike's needs, she went for a shower. Appropriate clothing? Dixie had never been in a gym in her life. A baggy pair of sweatpants and an oversized T-shirt were all she had to wear. The unflattering combination made her look as wide as she was tall. A slimline Dixie Mark Two? But what if the exercise routine *worked*? a more seductive voice asked, and she dawdled by the mirror then, imagining Scott suddenly recognising her as a member of the female sex...

Her stomach growling with hunger, she was about to go off in search of the kitchen when a quiet knock sounded on the door.

Fisher appeared with a tray bearing a tall glass filled with some strange greyish green liquid. 'Miss Stevens faxed your diet plan to Cook yesterday,' the butler explained. 'I believe this is the lady's own personal recipe for an early-morning energy boost.'

'Oh...' In bewilderment, Dixie accepted the glass. *Diet plan?* She didn't like the sound of that. She was willing to exercise, but diet? And who on earth was Fisher talking about?

'Miss Stevens?' Dixie queried with a frown.

'Gilda Stevens, the fitness instructor,' Fisher supplied expressionlessly. 'Her instructions regarding your menus were most precise.'

At that point, Dixie's tummy gave an embarrassing gurgle. So her fitness instructor was a woman. Taking a sip of the noxious brew, Dixie tried not to grimace. A cruel woman. The drink tasted like dishwater with bits of floating weed, but, remembering her manners, Dixie drank it down and waited eagerly to be told when she might receive her first meal of the day.

'Mr Valverde will be in the gym in five minutes,' the butler informed her as he retrieved the glass and returned to the door.

'What about breakfast? Do I eat later...or something?'

'That *was* breakfast, Miss Robinson.' At her aghast look of disbelief, the older man averted his eyes.

'A drink...a drink is all I'm allowed on this plan?' Dixie breathed shakily.

In silence, the older man nodded.

Fisher gave her directions to the gym. On her way there she caught tantalising glimpses of magnificent paintings, marble floors and wonderful rugs. She was not surprised to walk into a superb purpose-built gymnasium worthy of the most élite health club.

At the far end of the spacious room, César was lounging elegantly back against a piece of machinery that looked like an instrument for torture. He was talking to a brunette wearing less clothing than Dixie wore in bed. Presumably Gilda Stevens. A tiny white crop top adorned the lady's dainty bosom. Skintight white shorts hugged her impossibly slender hips. Every inch of visible skin was tanned and satin smooth.

Oh, no, why does she have to be so gorgeous? Dixie thought, cringing from such a cruel comparison, such an impossible peak of feminine perfection.

Tall and supremely authoritative in a dark designer suit, sunglasses dangling from one brown hand, César spoke without turning his dark, arrogant head. 'Don't skulk, Dixie. Come and join us. Gilda's done us a very special favor in agreeing to devote her personal attention to you at such short notice.'

The very thin brunette studied Dixie critically as she walked towards her.

Dixie flushed, her soft mouth tightening with embarrassment. César swivelled round, as light as a dancer on his feet in spite of his size. His winged brows pleated as he took in her appearance with frowning dark deepset eyes. 'Haven't you got anything more suitable to wear?'

'Dixie would probably feel too self-conscious in more revealing garments. I've seen this so many times before,' Gilda Stevens informed them both. 'Fortunately, diet and exercise can work real miracles—'

'Look...' Dixie began. 'I'm not an inanimate object you can discuss—'

'I'll send out for some gear for you,' César cut in, lean bronzed features already distant as he strode towards the door.

Gilda gave Dixie a cool, assessing appraisal from glassy blue eyes, and a panicky sensation twisted Dixie's empty tummy. Before she could even think about what she was doing, she raced in César Valverde's wake. Suddenly he felt like her only friend.

'César!' she gasped strickenly.

At the door he wheeled round, brilliant eyes glittering with impatience.

'César...she's not a normal woman,' Dixie whispered almost pleadingly. 'When she stands sideways on she's only about six inches wide! I didn't know anybody could be that thin and still live...and of course I look enormous to her, but I can't help the shape I was born with!'

After a stunned pause, César threw back his arrogant head and burst out laughing.

'It's not funny,' Dixic hissed in severe mortification. 'When you talked about hard work and effort, you didn't mention depriving me of food and putting a stick-insect in charge of me. Did you see how she looked at me? Like I was the size of an elephant and she wanted to skin me?'

César pivoted round to the wood-panelled wall and braced one lean hand against it as he struggled to contain his mirth. Turning his head back to her, silvered dark eyes still vibrant with reluctant amusement, he murmured drily, 'It's the deal, Dixie. Gilda has an international reputation in the fitness field.'

'I'm hungry,' Dixie mumbled tightly, but, disorientatingly, she found that she couldn't take her eyes off him. With laughter dying out of his lean, strong face and his cool, dark brooding air of detachment banished, she glimpsed a different César Valverde. A devastatingly masculine male with megawatt charisma, she recognised in some shock. Colouring with discomfiture, she dragged her eyes from him and stared at the wall instead.

'Tough...no pain, no gain,' César rhymed without pity.

'Have you ever been on a diet, César?' Out of the corner of her eye she could see his classic profile, and she found her head easing round towards him again without her own volition.

'I'm too disciplined to over-indulge.'

Dredging her attention from a profile worthy of a Greek sculptor, Dixie decided it would be safer to study the natural wood floor.

'Don't *do* that…it always winds me up!' César imparted with startling abruptness. 'Look at me when I'm speaking to you!'

Blinking in hot-faced bewilderment that he had actually noticed she almost never looked directly at him, Dixie glanced up.

César's aggressive jawline eased only slightly. 'That's only one of your most annoying habits.'

As he turned away, Dixie cleared her throat awkwardly. 'What did you tell Miss Stevens to explain *why* you are hiring her for my benefit?'

Complete surprise flared in his stunning eyes. 'I don't explain my actions to anyone. Why should I?'

Why should I? The baseline on the way César Valverde lived his entire life, Dixie registered. He was so self-contained, so unapologetic about guarding his privacy. Naturally he wouldn't have the slightest inhibition about snubbing people who exercised their curiosity.

'Dixie…we'd better get started,' Gilda Stevens called. 'We'll begin with a weigh-in.'

Dixie hadn't been on the scales since she was sixteen, and inside herself she simply cowered.

'I'll see you tomorrow,' Gilda told Dixie.

Face-down on a mat, perspiring freely, Dixie tried to nod, but even that took muscle power and she decided not to bother. After all, at some stage she would have to get up, walk…well, maybe crawl, she decided. She was beyond caring about putting a proud face on her exhaustion.

'You're out of condition,' her torturer sighed as she took her leave. 'But now I've shown you the ropes you'll be able to follow through on your own every day.'

Every day. Dixie suppressed a groan but she forced a grateful smile. Gilda might be tough, pitiless and completely lacking in the humour department, but she had worked out alongside her and had been tireless in her efforts to ensure that Dixie did every single exercise correctly. Horribly, hatefully tireless.

Left alone, Dixie slowly slid into a comfortable doze. The sound of footsteps made her stir. Tipping back her head, she focused sleepily on Fisher's polished shoes.

'Where would you like to eat lunch?' the butler asked.

'Here will do.'

A tray was set on the floor. A plate piled high with salad greens and raw slivers of vegetable awaited her.

'I never liked salad,' Dixie confided guiltily.

'It's a detoxifying diet, I believe,' Fisher commented. 'You do get a whole grapefruit mid-afternoon.'

Dixie's tastebuds shuddered, but she was so hungry she munched at a piece of celery. 'I like starchy food. I like meat, pasta with lashings of cheese...chocolate fudge cake,' she enumerated longingly, mouth watering as she fantasised.

Another pair of shoes appeared in her field of vision. Italian leather casuals with handstitched seams. She froze.

'But you're not allowed to cheat,' César Valverde drawled.

'I thought you were at the bank,' Dixie said accusingly.

'I intend to keep an eye on this project. Just as well,' César condemned. 'Gilda's gone, and here you are lazing about like you're on holiday!'

'I'm so weak I can't move!' Dixie gasped in disbelief.

César crouched down to her level with athletic ease. Hard dark eyes assailed her dismayed orbs in a head-on collision. 'I checked your staff medical. You're healthy. There's no reason why you shouldn't follow a structured fitness regime. Why didn't you change into one of the exercise outfits I had sent over?'

They had all looked so incredibly small, and Dixie hadn't fancied struggling to squeeze herself into figure-hugging garments with Gilda around.

'You're over-tired because you let yourself get far too hot.'

'I need to eat to have energy,' Dixie muttered self-pityingly.

César dealt her a chilling glance of reproof. 'Your attitude to this is all wrong. In fact your attitude to life in general is your biggest flaw. You're so convinced you're going to fail you won't even bother trying!'

'I'll follow the schedule...OK?'

'That's not good enough. I want one hundred and five per cent commitment from you.' As César studied her with fulminating intensity, his jawline squared. 'Keep in mind what this is costing me. The sum total of your debts was considerable. And if you haven't learnt it yet, learn it now. There is no such thing as a free lunch.'

Having paled during that crushing speech, Dixie could no longer meet his ruthlessly intent gaze. 'I...I—'

'I paid for the right to expect you to stick to your side of this deal. Start slacking and you'll have me standing over you with a stopwatch! And if you think Gilda's bad, you ain't seen nothing yet!' César swore in unapologetic threat.

That evening, Scott's welcoming, 'Am I glad to see you!' was balm to Dixie's low self-esteem when she arrived on his doorstep.

Shyly pushing her heavy fringe off her brow, Dixie smiled up at him. Tall, slim and fair-haired, Scott responded with a matey punch that hurt her shoulder, and showed her straight into his kitchen.

'I had some friends staying for a couple of days. What a mess they left this place in!' he complained.

'I'll soon have it sorted out,' Dixie told him eagerly.

On his way back out again, Scott glanced at her and then frowned slightly. Pausing in the doorway, he stared at her. 'Have you done something to your hair or changed your make-up or something?'

Dixie tensed. 'No...I don't wear make-up.'

'It must be the colour in your cheeks. You look almost pretty.' Scott shook his handsome head over this apparently amazing development, frowned as if he was rather surprised to have noticed the fact, and departed, leaving her to the mounds of dishes stacked on every available surface.

Almost pretty. In real shock at the very first compliment Scott had ever deigned to pay her, Dixie hovered in the centre of his filthy kitchen with a dreamy look on her face. Colour in her cheeks? It was the effect of the exercise, it *had* to be! Maybe the detoxifying diet was starting to work already! Scott had finally noticed that she was female...

Suddenly feeling like a woman on a mission that might just miraculously transform her life, Dixie swore to herself that she would be up early the next day and into the gym to work out. Humming happily, she washed dishes, scrubbed the floor and cleaned the cooker.

'I don't know how you do it!' Scott exclaimed appreciatively as he paused by the kitchen door in the act of donning the jacket of a smart suit. 'What would I do without you, Dixie?'

Like a starved plant suddenly plunged into water and sunlight, Dixie blossomed and beamed at him.

'I'm off out now, but there's no need for you to hurry home,' Scott assured her. 'And if you could find the time to run the vacuum cleaner round the sitting room, I'd be really grateful.'

'No problem,' Dixie hurried to tell him. 'Is the washing machine fixed yet?'

'No, the mechanic's coming on Wednesday.' Scott grimaced. 'He says I must have one of those rogue machines.'

Dixie followed him to his front door with the aspect of someone walking on hallowed ground. 'Hot date?' she asked with laden casualness.

'Yeah. A real stunner too,' Scott chuckled. 'See you, Dixie!'

'See you,' she whispered, closing the door in his wake.

It was after ten when Dixie and Spike got back to César Valverde's imposing home. She had to use the front door and press the bell to gain entry. She just hadn't been able to bring herself to leave Scott's apartment sooner, not until she had polished every piece of furniture and vacuumed every inch of carpet. As Fisher said goodnight to her, Dixie gave him a vague smile and drifted away.

She was ludicrously unprepared for César Valverde to stride out of one of the reception rooms off the lofty ceilinged hall and demand harshly, 'Where the hell have you been?'

'I...I b-beg your pardon?' Dixie stammered.

'I expected a report on your progress at six and you'd already gone out,' César imparted grimly.

'Oh...I was with Scott.' Dixie studied him vaguely, as if she couldn't quite manage to get him into focus. In fact, she was striving to superimpose Scott's beloved features onto César, to make him more bearable, but for some strange reason the attempt wasn't working. And instead she somehow found herself making all sorts of foolish comparisons between the two men...

César was much taller, more powerfully built, his skin a vibrant gold where Scott's was fair. César's luxuriant black hair was perfectly cut to his well-shaped head, not endearingly floppy like Scott's...oh, heavens, what was she doing, and why was she studying César Valverde like this, noticing every tiny thing about him where once she had been afraid to look at him?

An odd shivery sensation Dixie had never experienced before ran through her when she collided with those striking dark eyes of his...so piercing, so brilliant, so *alive*. A definable five o'clock shadow roughened his jawline, accentuating the wide, sensual shape of his mouth, the perfect whiteness of his teeth. And he still looked so incredibly, impossibly immaculate, she reflected in growing wonderment. How did he *do* it? Here she was, with wind-tousled damp hair, a stain of cleansing fluid on her T-shirt and shoes spattered from puddles.

'How do you do it...how do you look so perfect all the time?' Dixie heard herself ask wistfully, desperate for the magic secret, the miracle formula which might transform her appearance as well.

'Are we on the same planet?' César enquired with satiric bite.

'I don't think so.' Dixie reddened with sudden discomfiture.

'Who's Scott? A boyfriend?' César demanded with a chilling edge to his dark, deep-accented voice.

'Oh, I don't have a boyfriend… Scott's just… Scott…well, Scott…' Suddenly Dixie was having some difficulty in quantifying her relationship with Scott, because tonight she had rediscovered hope, and to write Scott off as merely a friend now felt like acknowledging defeat again.

'Scott?' César queried with an impatient flare of one ebony brow.

'Scott Lewis…' Her blue eyes became even more abstracted. 'I love him, but he hasn't really noticed me that way yet, but I think he might be on the brink—'

César clenched his even white teeth. 'I'm getting closer to the brink too—'

Dixie heaved a sigh, shoulders down-curving. 'So I suppose I still have to say that Scott's just a friend.'

'Dixie…I asked a straight question. I didn't request an outpouring of girlish confidence,'

César informed her with withering cool. 'I hope you're more circumspect with him than you are with me. I don't expect to find out that you've confided in him about our private arrangement.'

'Scott and I don't have those kind of conversations.' Inexplicably the happy shine on Dixie's evening was now beginning to drain away, leaving her feeling rather down on the dumps. 'Nothing deep—'

'He's got his head screwed on, then, hasn't he?' César sent her a winging glance of burning exasperation. 'You're not grounded enough for a deep conversation. Inside that flighty, vacant head of yours, you're up in the bloody clouds with the angels most of the time!'

But then there was no room for magic or love in César Valverde's world. He was so grounded in reality he didn't know what it was to dream. Well, he was missing out on an awful lot, Dixie decided, determined not to be affected by his censure.

Without warning the door of the room César had emerged from opened again. A gorgeous blonde in an elegant strappy black dress peered out and frowned at Dixie. 'Staff problems, César?'

Taken aback by the appearance of the other woman, Dixie stiffened with discomfiture.

César dredged his frustrated attention from Dixie and turned with a slashing smile. 'Nothing that need concern you, Lisette.'

Lisette. Frisky name for a frisky lady, Dixie thought nastily, and then was genuinely shocked by her own bitchiness. Lisette was probably a very nice woman, and was undoubtedly far too good for César Valverde. He was a real rat, the kind of guy who didn't phone, always put work first, cancelled dates last-minute and strayed without conscience the instant he got bored. Poor Lisette. She was more to be pitied.

Dixie went to her room and settled Spike into his basket. She fed César the goldfish, still feeling guilty about him being alone in his bowl. But he obviously preferred being alone. He was an aggressive fish. But possibly the two companions he had eaten had been the wrong sex, she reflected with a considering frown. Maybe he would be transformed by the arrival of a female fish... Could she risk adding to the body count?

As Dixie pulled on her shortie pyjamas, she struggled against the conviction that if she didn't eat some proper food soon her stomach would meet her backbone. After all, now she had a goal, a *real* goal. Scott was worth that one hundred and five per cent commitment César had demanded from her. She would throw herself heart and soul into Gilda's fitness schedule.

But hunger kept Dixie tossing and turning, unable to sleep. At one in the morning she rolled out of bed in sudden decision. An apple, a slice of toast, a cup of tea with the merest drop of milk…surely such a meagre snack wouldn't show on the scales?

As Dixie crept with a fast-bating heart towards the kitchen, the entire house was in darkness. She stubbed her toe on the edge of the kitchen door and went hopping round on one leg in the gloom, silently screaming until the worst of the pain receded. Then she folded down on her knees in front of the giant fridge. Tugging open the door, she sat there gently massaging her aching toe and contemplating the immensity of the temptation now available.

One little sin, she urged herself circumspectly. Just one… A sandwich…she wouldn't butter the bread, she bargained with herself. Or what about a thin slice of cheese on toast with a dash of that salsa…or possibly…?

'Just what do you think you're playing at?'

At the sound of that raw-edged icy demand coming out of nowhere at her, Dixie almost had a heart attack.

CHAPTER THREE

WITH a strangled cry of fright, Dixie twisted round on her knees, her heart pounding so fast she couldn't breathe.

The lights beneath the units flipped on, framing César, barefoot and bare-chested, only a pair of close-fitting jeans hugging his long, powerful legs as he stood there surveying her with complete scorn.

'I only wanted a little snack,' Dixie whispered tremulously. 'I didn't think I'd wake anybody up!'

'When I go to bed, I switch on the alarm system. If anything moves down here, I know about it.'

Abstractedly still rubbing at her throbbing toe, Dixie studied him with huge violet eyes. Clothed he was intimidating; half-naked he was...he was *awesome*. The instant that thought occurred to her, she reddened with mortification and twisted her head away, terrified that he might read her face and somehow *know* what she'd been thinking. But in her mind's eye she still saw César. Wide brown shoulders, sleek strong muscles flexing beneath smooth healthy skin as his hand dropped back from the light switch, a magnificent torso with curling black hair hazing his pectorals, and a stomach as taut and flat as a washboard.

A frisson of strange heat curled in Dixie's stomach and then seemed to dart down somewhere infinitely more private and sort of twist in pleasure-pain. Her mouth felt as dry as a bone and she didn't know what was the matter with her. Spooked by his descent, and dying with embarrassment at being caught in the act of trying to cheat on her diet plan, it was all too much at once. Dixie parted her lips to explain herself, but to her utter horror a choky little sob escaped instead.

'*Porca miseria!*' César glowered at her in disbelief. 'You can't be *that* hungry!'

Seeing him through a haze of mortifying tears, Dixie dragged herself upright and turned away, struggling to get a grip on her seesawing emotions and hide her face.

She didn't read anything into the silence that followed, merely pictured him gripping his whiplash tongue between his teeth sooner than risk provoking her into a real crying jag. And she felt so hatefully childish. She had never been a crybaby, but he always made her feel so awkward, useless and silly.

'*Madre di Dio…*' César Valverde breathed incredulously. 'Who ever would have believed it? You've got the body of a men's magazine centrefold!'

Dixie's damp eyes slowly opened wide with bewilderment. Not even crediting that he could possibly have said what she thought he had said, she whirled round. She connected with stunned dark eyes engaged in a shockingly intimate appraisal of her lightly clad length. Having until that instant completely overlooked the fact that she was only wearing a pair of shrunken shortie pyjamas, Dixie crimsoned under that raking scrutiny and crossed her arms over herself.

'Don't!' César ejaculated forcefully, his seemingly mesmerised attention nailed to the proud swell of her full breasts so clearly delineated by the clinging cotton jersey.

His transfixed gaze came to a halt at her tiny waist, and at that point keeping a distance became more than he could apparently bear. Striding over to her, he turned her round with one impatient hand. Like a male quite unable to believe the evidence of his own eyes, he scanned the highly feminine curve of her hips and the surprising length of her shapely legs.

'What…for heavens' sake…*what are you doing*?' she gasped in helpless confusion at his behavior as she attempted to coil away and conceal as much as possible of the body she loathed.

'I assumed you were overweight. I thought you were hiding a multitude of sins beneath those shapeless sacky clothes you wore. I didn't even know you *had* a waist! And *Dio*, all the time…all the time,' César slowly repeated in a roughened and dazed undertone that sent a curious quiver rippling down her taut backbone, 'You were covering up the kind of lush curves that keep teenage boys awake and fantasising at night!'

'I don't know what you're talking about!' Dixie pulled away, hugging herself with her arms, shaken and mortified by what he was saying and convinced that he was being sarcastic. But, whatever, it was obvious that in his eyes she wasn't anything like as overweight as he had evidently believed she was. So maybe she could now risk letting her breath out, because holding her stomach in was becoming painful.

César backed off a soundless step, brilliant dark eyes veiled, faint colour highlighting his slashing cheekbones. A shuttered look wiped all expression from his stunning dark features as he continued to survey her. 'I know you don't. And while obviously you have no idea how to maximise what you've got, *I* have,' he stressed with unconcealed satisfaction. 'We'll be in Spain within a few days.'

'Within a few days?' Dixie parroted in astonishment. 'But that doesn't give me enough time to—'

'You don't need time. All you need is the right clothes and something done with that hideous untidy mop of Raggedy-Ann curls.' César strolled gracefully over to the fridge, flipped the door wide and cast her a satiric glance. 'Eat your heart out! And go easy on the exercise. Conserve your potential. I intend to exploit every luscious inch.'

And with that smooth invitation, light gleaming over his thick dark hair and smooth brown back, César sauntered back out of the kitchen, exuding in waves the kind of self-satisfied aura that he usually reserved for closing a major deal.

Every luscious inch? In a total daze of disbelief, Dixie squinted down at the much despised bountiful bosom which had caused her such agonies of mortification during her teens. Both her stepmother, Muriel, and Petra had been naturally thin, and only minimally endowed in that department. Both had fully entered into Dixie's conviction that such generous curves were gross and only worthy of concealment.

And school had been a nightmare for Dixie. She had started to develop at an age when her classmates were still flat-chested. The cruel, thoughtless teasing from the girls and the crude comments of the rowdier boys had devastated

Dixie's confidence in her own body. Her pronounced hour-glass shape had made her a target for ridicule. Times without number she had come home from school and gone up to her room to cry her heart out.

Muriel had bought her a big sloppy sweater which she could pull down over her hips, ensuring that the size of her breasts became instantly less likely to attract attention. And ever since then Dixie had relied on the same remedy and dressed accordingly.

And yet César Valverde had, incredible as it seemed to her, actually looked at her figure with stunned appreciation. No, not any kind of *personal* appreciation, she hurriedly adjusted, wondering how on earth she had contrived to pick up such an exaggerated false impression from him. He had only been acknowledging that she had the sort of over-generous curves that teenage boys liked, and that was certainly not news to Dixie. His appreciation had been of the entirely dispassionate variety. But what she had always considered a great disadvantage and a flaw, César somehow saw as an asset.

And suddenly he didn't think she needed to lose weight, or even exercise too much. But had she really stood there, letting him look her over when she was, if not quite half-naked, certainly only minimally clad? A hot tide of painful color swept up Dixie's throat at that belated awareness. He had taken her so much by surprise. Now she felt sick with chagrin, and all desire to eat had ironically evaporated. Slamming shut the fridge door, she returned to her room.

So César Valverde didn't think she was quite as unattractive as he had believed. Hadn't he noticed her tummy or the surplus flesh on her thighs and ribcage? She peered over her shoulder at the pronounced swell of her hips and slowly shook her head, his staggering change in attitude still a complete mystery to her. But then César Valverde treated her like a piece of meat, to be properly packaged for sale in a butcher's window, and after all, the only living person she had to impress was Jasper Dysart...

César walked into the sunlit gym with Gilda the next morning and then stopped dead. His sunglasses dropped out clean of his hand. Sheathed in a fitting one-piece dark green leotard, Dixie was doing her warm-up exercises.

She paused and connected unexpectedly with César's shimmering dark eyes. She fiercely resisted the urge to wrap her arms round herself like a self-conscious schoolgirl. The leotard was less revealing than a swimsuit, she reminded herself. As she gazed across the gym, unwittingly entrapped by that piercing silvered stare of his, so bright in that dark masculine face, she began feeling light-headed, and without even realising it slowly fell still.

A wave of startling heat slowly engulfed her from head to toe. Her eyes widened, her pupils dilating as for the first time she became aware of her own body in the most extraordinarily unsettling way. Her skin felt too hot and tight to encase her bones. Her breasts felt strangely heavy, stirring in their cotton casing with her every shortened breath and making her nipples ache with oversensitivity.

Gilda picked up César's sunglasses and extended them to him. With a slight frown he slowly dredged his attention from Dixie, and momentarily studied the sunglasses as if they didn't belong to him.

'I got up really early this morning.' Dixie blinked rapidly, like a sleepwalker rudely awakened. She folded her arms tightly above her waist, face burning as she strove to work out what had happened to her there for a few seconds while seriously hoping it never, ever happened again because she had felt really peculiar.

'That's the spirit!' Gilda applauded in the incredibly tense silence.

Without comment, César strolled over to one of the tall windows, effortlessly elegant in pale, beautifully cut chinos and an aqua silk short-sleeved shirt. Dixie's gaze abstractedly followed him, taking in the tense set of his wide shoulders, the aggressive jut of his set profile and the dusting of darker colour delineating one carved cheekbone. He was so incredibly perfect, she conceded absently, still having a problem getting her brain into gear while she could not help but wonder what was bothering him. Business, no doubt, or perhaps irritation at her unwelcome presence in his home and the disruption of his own workaholic schedule.

Two days later, Dixie appraised her new hairstyle in fascination. Her mop of curls had been tamed by the talented stylist. Sleek, feathery layers curved back from her face, fanning down into casual waves just clear of her shoulders. Shorn of the chunky overhang of hair she used to hide behind, her cheekbones now lent fresh definition to her features.

The beautician was waiting for her in another part of the salon. Dixie had given up on make-up because she had always seemed to buy the wrong colours and had never been satisfied with the look she ended up with. But with an expert adviser on hand to select the right shades, she was delighted with the subtle effect contrived with a few light cosmetics.

Clutching a beauty case crammed with items, as per César's explicit instructions, she finally emerged and walked back to the waiting area. She was astonished to see César there, talking into a mobile phone while glancing broodingly at his watch and studiously ignoring the many languishing female glances coming his way from both staff and customers.

Dixie's steps slowed. Look at me, she suddenly wanted to shout. *Notice* me! The shock of that instant desire to impress was profound, but she soon explained it to her own satisfaction. Five minutes after she had arrived for her appointment at the salon, César had descended without warning. So wasn't it only natural that he should now be keen to see the end result, and equally natural that she should expect to be noticed?

After all, hadn't he told the stylist exactly what he wanted him to do with her hair? Hadn't he warned the beautician that he didn't want her covered in what he had bluntly described as 'a two-inch deep layer of goop'? She smiled helplessly at the memory.

'You've got to have a tongue in your head in a place like this,' César had informed her drily before he departed again. '*You'd* give them a free hand, but they need limits.'

And Dixie hadn't been the slightest bit embarrassed while César was domineeringly engaged in setting those limits, because two most unexpected compliments had indirectly come her way. No, Dixie would not require highlights, lowlights or any other kind of lights in her dark brown hair. Dark brown hair was elegant, César had stated, and also, since Dixie had flawless skin, why cover it up?

Now, when she was about six feet away from him, César's smooth dark head turned in her direction. He stilled, appraising her with unreadable dark-as-night eyes. Her breath fluttered in her throat, her heartbeat quickening as she waited for his reaction.

'Major improvement,' César commented as he retracted the aerial on his mobile and strode towards the exit, having awarded her little more than an assessing glance.

The wobbly smile of anticipation on Dixie's lips fell away as she rushed to keep up with him. 'Yes, it is, isn't it?'

'What?'

'An improvement?' Dixie reminded him wistfully, encouragingly, as they emerged on to the crowded street outside. 'I can't believe I look so much smarter.'

'Only from the neck up. Your wardrobe is still a disaster area,' César pointed out, thoroughly deflating her as he stood back for her to step into the rear of his chauffeur-driven limousine.

'No, you first,' she urged uncomfortably, still very conscious of what she felt to be his superior status.

'Move, Dixie,' César gritted in her ear.

In haste, Dixie scrambled into the limousine, sending a file sitting on the back seat flying. As documents spilled out, Dixie groaned and bent down to clumsily gather them up again. 'I didn't expect you to take the trouble to come into the salon this morning,' she admitted, squinting down at the documents and realising that there was no way she could even try to put them back in order when they were written in a foreign language.

'I didn't expect to have to take the trouble either,' César confided almost to himself, his attention lingering fixedly on the mess of confused papers now being apologetically slid on to the seat between them. 'I was in the middle of a board meeting before it dawned on me that I couldn't trust you alone in a place like that. You might go overboard and emerge looking totally unrecognisable—'

'I've always sort of wanted to be blonde,' Dixie mused absently, now engaged in hurriedly cramming the documents out of sight within the file. 'My sister's blonde—'

'—or you'd sit there in a total daydream and let them do whatever they felt like doing to you. It was too big a risk.'

'I'm sure this has all been very inconvenient for you,' Dixie muttered ruefully.

'You're not joking, but we'll get the clothes problem sorted today too. We're flying out to Spain the day after tomorrow.'

'That soon?' Dixie sighed. 'Spike's going to miss me terribly.'

'The dog? I haven't laid eyes on that dog since the night you moved in,' César remarked, with belated awareness of that surprising fact.

'Oh, you have, you just haven't noticed him. Spike hides when there are people around. He was very badly treated by his first owner. The lady he used to stay with during the day was a volunteer at the animal refuge, but he'll have to stay in your house while I'm away because I couldn't ask her to keep him for so long.'

'Couldn't…er…Scott keep him?'

'Spike is terrified of men. Anyway, Scott's at work all day, and often out at night as well. I'm going to miss him too… Do you think I'll be in Spain long?' she asked rather guiltily.

'What does Scott do?' César enquired, without answering that question.

'He's a stockbroker with a City firm called Lyle and something…'

'Makes sense,' César said softly.

'What does?'

'That the smartass who has you acting as an unpaid skivvy would be a broker. Brokers are wheeler-dealers. He saw you coming.' César flicked her a narrowed glance of complete exasperation.

'You don't know what you're talking about... Scott is *not* a smartass!' Dixie had turned very pink, highly disconcerted as she was by that uninvited opinion coming from such a source.

'He knows that you're infatuated with him and he uses it to his own advantage.'

'I didn't ask you what you think and I don't want to know either!' Her hands tightly linked on her lap, Dixie stared unseeingly out the window at the heavy traffic. 'How did you find out that I help out with his housework anyway?' She suddenly had to know.

'I heard two of the secretaries talking about what an idiot you were weeks ago.'

Dixie trembled. It took that much effort to hold in the surge of angry humiliation now eating her alive.

'You don't seem to know any of the tricks other women are *born* knowing. Doing the guy's washing doesn't seem to be getting you very far,' César said with scathing cool.

'I hate you...do you know that?' Dixie jerked round to look at him, violet eyes pools of angry, hurt reproach.

'For telling you the truth? If you had any decent friends they'd have broken the news and given you a few useful hints long ago.'

For a split second meeting those stunning dark eyes on the level deprived Dixie of both breath and concentration. Her lashes fluttered in confusion and her head whirled. She sucked in oxygen and hurriedly turned her head away again, her heart slamming hard against her breastbone. She felt really shaky in the aftermath of that exchanged glance, and blamed it on her overtaxed emotions.

'You think I'm wasting my time, and yet you don't know Scott and you don't know me. What sort of ''useful hints'' do you think I need?'

'*Dio*...I'm not an agony aunt,' César drawled, boredom oozing from every honeyed accented syllable.

'Jasper spoilt you terribly...' Dixie's chagrined reaction to that snub leapt straight on to her tongue. 'That's why he worries about you so much. He feels responsible for the way you've turned out!'

The silence that rewarded that startling speech positively reverberated in her ears. Realising that she had been inexcusably blunt on the worst possible subject, Dixie glanced up in stricken apprehension.

Outraged dark eyes filled with rampant incredulity were trained to her.

'I'm sorry. I was too personal…but it's just you can be so very rude, and it doesn't seem to bother you that other people have feelings that can be hurt,' Dixie completed shakily.

'Is that a fact?' César drawled, with a sardonic smile that utterly dismissed her comments.

But Dixie was not fooled. She had drawn blood. His fabulous bone structure was rigid, his eyes glittering hard as diamonds. Dixie bent her head, shaken that she had spoken up to censure him and conscious that she had struck a very low and inappropriate blow in revealing that his godfather had actually discussed such very personal concerns with her.

She was thoroughly ashamed of herself. How could she have been so thoughtless? How could she have betrayed Jasper's confidence? And even though he had never been known to show them, César *had* to have some feelings! Naturally she had hurt César by voicing Jasper's guilty conviction that he had made serious parenting mistakes while he was his guardian.

Jasper had told her that César had always inhabited another plane from his peers. Intellectual brilliance had set him apart at an early age and made him intolerant of those less able. That whiplash tongue had made people very scared of César Valverde. If they weren't super-careful they lost face in César's presence; scorn was infinitely more humiliating than a straightforward rebuke or criticism.

'I should never have said those things,' Dixie whispered valiantly, desperately needing to try and put right any damage she might have done, particularly to Jasper's standing in César's highly critical eyes. 'And you mustn't get the idea that Jasper discussed you with me—'

'Where would I get an idea like that?' César countered, with such tacit scorn that she paled with even greater dismay and guilt.

'But it wasn't like that!' Dixie protested frantically. 'You remember all the publicity there was about that actress you dumped last summer? The one who was rushed into hospital with an overdose—?'

'Not an overdose. Alcoholic poisoning.'

'Oh...w-was it really?' Dixie floundered at that immediate contradiction.

'I dumped her because she was never sober,' César returned icily.

'Jasper didn't kn-know that, and he was upset at all the furore in the papers,' Dixie stammered. 'And that was when he said just a few things *unthinkingly*,' she stressed feverishly, 'about the way he had brought you up not having been the best—'

'*Accidenti!* I only knew the woman a few weeks.' Black eyes assailed hers in remorseless challenge. 'She had a problem long before I met her, but I persuaded her to accept professional help *and* I arranged for her to stay in a special unit where she received all the counselling and support she needed.'

'J-Jasper would've been so relieved to know all that,' Dixie mumbled weakly, treading now on ground she wished she had never dared to set a single toe upon.

Indeed, now squirming with embarrassment over her own clumsy misapprehensions, Dixie felt ten times worse. When she climbed out of the limo in César's imperious wake, she put an anxious hand on his sleeve. From his lofty height, he studied her small hand as if it was a gross invasion of his personal space.

Her nerveless fingers slid off his sleeve again as though she had been burnt. 'I didn't mean to hurt your feelings.' Sincere concern shone from her scrutiny.

'Hurt my feelings?' César echoed in disbelief. 'Where the hell do you get the idea that—?'

'You're a not very easy person to apologise to…are you?' Dixie was appalled to see bitter anger flaming in his burnished dark eyes. 'I just seem to keep on digging myself into a deeper hole with you. Every time I open my mouth, I put my foot in it.'

'A vow of silence would be welcome,' César spelt out grittily.

She got on his nerves, she conceded, her shoulders slumping.

'Don't slouch.' A lean hand squared over her spine to brace her upright again.

He really disliked her, Dixie thought morosely. Everything she did and said irritated him. She wasn't used to being disliked. Presumably that was why she felt so absolutely awful all of a sudden. Her usually sunny nature reacted to the endless night of his like oil on water. They were such incompatible personalities. He was so cold, so unfeeling, so critical, and that made her more nervous, more likely to say and do the wrong thing. She had always found it totally impossible to concentrate around César Valverde. It was as if her brain went on holiday.

César stole an undeniably apprehensive glance down at her tremulous lip line.

'I'm not going to cry…I'm *not*!' Dixie swore.

'You're not convincing me.'

Her wide eyes shimmered.

'*Dio*…you have really stunning eyes,' César breathed in an abrupt and roughened undertone, staring down into her face as if she was the only woman in the universe.

In severe shock, Dixie gazed back up at him, even her breathing arrested. That deep, sexy, accented drawl rippled down her sensitive spine and made her shiver in reaction. Locked into the dense darkness of his amazing eyes, it was as if the world had stopped turning for her, sentencing her to paralysis. Not a single thought filled her blank mind. And yet on another level she dimly recognised the desperate yearning surging up inside her like a hungry, terrifying beast. That sensation scared the living daylights out of her, but still she couldn't have moved, couldn't have spoken, couldn't have broken the spell that held her fast.

César did that. While she gazed at him, her heart beating so fast it felt as if it was about to burst from her chest, his spiky glossy black lashes lowered, setting her free from the cage of her own suffocating excitement. And as she watched, trembling, utterly disorientated by what was happening to her, she saw him breathe in very slowly and deeply, like a male tasting life-giving air after a long time asleep. A black frown line indented his brow, his striking features broodingly tense for a split second.

'I just got this really creepy feeling,' Dixie confided helplessly, tottering away from him to

cannon blindly into a group of shoppers and stop
to splutter unsought apologies while still blocking their path.

'Really…creepy…feeling?' César framed expressionlessly as he reached out a lean brown
hand and tugged her out of harm's way and back
towards him.

'I'm not feeling very well.' Her body still running alternately hot and cold like a broken boiler,
her head spinning, her legs weak as matchsticks
and her breasts throbbing in the most mortifying
and uncomfortable way, Dixie focused on his
burgundy silk tie with big bewildered eyes. 'I
hope it's not the flu…or maybe I'm upset because I'm not likely to see Scott again for ages.'

A vague frown of recall on her flushed face,
she looked up at César, surprised by the intensity
of his piercing gaze. 'Why did you say that about
my eyes?'

'I was trying to distract you. It worked like
magic.' His eyes were as remote and icy as the
Himalayas.

Distract her? From what? Oh, the tears. He had
thought she was about to burst into tears and embarrass him in public. Naturally the bit about her
eyes being stunning had been a whopper. It was
a wonder he had managed to keep his face
straight while he said it.

César urged her through the gilded doors of the hugely impressive store they had been standing outside. One step inside the doors, he abandoned her. The silence of an élite clientele and very expensive merchandise intimidated Dixie.

Her attention stayed with César, now in close conversation with a svelte older woman who appeared to have been awaiting their arrival. César had the most weird effect on her, she mused. That almost sick sensation of excitement she could only equate to her never-to-be-forgotten terror on a rollercoaster ride as a child. And he had treated her like an overwrought child.

He strode back across the floor to her, looking every inch what he was. A very, very rich and powerful man, a highly sophisticated male, superbly elegant in a formal pinstripe suit that accentuated every powerful line of his lean, magnificent length. He stopped a good four feet from her, rather as if he was in the presence of potential contagion. His expression was cold and hard as stone.

'Mariah will select your clothes. Regard them as props and don't question her judgement. She knows what I want.'

And with that icy assurance he took his leave. Dixie stared after him with a perplexed frown. What had she done to deserve the deep freeze treatment? Just been herself, she decided glumly.

Tactless, clumsy and embarrassingly emotional. Three flaws that César would never suffer from.

The evening of the following day, Dixie cast a dubious glance at herself in the bedroom mirror. Was that really her? The blue chambray skirt and fitted jacket showed an awful lot more of her body than she was used to seeing. As for the silk T-shirt she wore beneath, every time she looked down she was confronted by a view of her own cleavage. The strappy stiletto shoes had perilously high heels and she found it hard to walk in them.

The phone by her bed buzzed and she answered it.

'I want to see you in the drawing room in ten minutes,' César drawled coolly.

'Gosh, you nearly missed me. I was just on my way out to Scott's,' she confided cheerfully.

'It's going to take me a while to get the hang of these heels,' she carolled as she stumbled in the drawing room doorway and had to snatch at the doorhandle to steady herself.

In the act of lifting a brandy goblet to his lips, César froze. Dixie froze too. He was wearing a white dinner jacket that fitted him like a glove, the light colour throwing his vibrant golden skin and black hair and dark eyes into exotic prominence. He looked so devastatingly attractive Dixie's soft mouth fell open.

And for some reason César was staring at her too. Suddenly self-conscious, and mortified by the way she had gaped at him, Dixie got all hot and bothered. 'Is this going to take long? I don't want to miss Scott.'

'*Dio mio*…he's unlikely to miss you.' Brilliant dark eyes scanned the fit of the T-shirt, the skirt outlining her tiny waist, then dropped to the shapely legs on display outside the gym for the first time. 'That bloody stupid woman!' he grated abruptly. 'You look like a bimbo! That neckline's too low. That skirt is too short.'

In frank dismay and surprise, Dixie gazed back at him. 'The skirt's only three inches above my knee—'

'Totally inappropriate for Jasper…and even more inappropriate for doing Scott's washing,' César completed with withering bite.

'I wanted him to see my new look.' Dixie's face had fallen like a disappointed child's.

César elevated a winged ebony brow, and suddenly such a desire seemed pathetic on her part. She flushed miserably.

Feeling both over and under-dressed, Dixie relinquished the colourful fantasy of Scott taking one look at her and instantly realising that she was the woman for him. She would put on her usual clothes and remove the make-up. Suddenly she was grateful that César had spoken up. She didn't want to make it obvious to Scott that she was trying to attract him. That might wreck their friendship and scare him off altogether, mightn't it?

'A jeweller is coming to show us a selection of engagement rings.'

'Oh…' Dixie said.

'Whatever you pick you can keep,' César informed her carelessly.

'No. When I get a *real* engagement ring, I'd like it to be my first. I'll just look on this one as being on loan.'

The jeweller arrived. By then, Dixie was hunched on the sofa, looking very self-conscious. She so wished she had had time to get changed. César was a real sophisticate, and if he thought she was showing too much flesh obviously he had to be right. She was ashamed that he had had to tell her what she should have realised for herself. And yet she had seen loads and loads of perfectly respectable young women wearing what she had assumed were similar clothes.

But now her jacket was buttoned to her throat, to conceal the offending T-shirt, and her restive fingers were constantly tugging at the hem of the skirt which felt indecently short.

'So choose,' César invited in the increasingly tense silence.

'Diamonds are very cold,' Dixie sighed. 'Pearls and opals are unlucky. Some people say green isn't very lucky either. I don't know anything bad about rubies, *but*—'

'So pick a ruby.'

The jeweller, who was keeping his head down, hurriedly extended the appropriate tray.

'Rubies are supposed to stand for passionate love,' Dixie completed in an apologetic undertone. 'A diamond might be more suitable.'

César breathed in very deep. With an unerring eye, he reached down to select the most opulent diamond ring. 'We'll have this one.'

The cluster was so big it looked like a fake out of a Christmas cracker. Dixie was relieved that she didn't like the ring. She felt it kept everything on a comfortingly impersonal basis.

As soon as the jeweller had checked the size of her finger, Dixie was on her feet. 'Can I go now?'

'Please don't let me keep you,' César drawled acidly.

Thirty minutes later, Dixie rang Scott's doorbell. She was totally taken aback when the door was answered by an unfamiliar man.

'Looking for Scott?' he said helpfully.

Dixie nodded.

'We work together...he said I could use this place while he's in New York.'

'New York?' Dixie stressed in a shaken tone, certain she must have misunderstood.

'Temporary secondment. Scott only got the offer yesterday. A chance like that, he didn't waste any time. He flew out this morning.'

Dixie was in shock. 'How long is he likely to be away?'

'A couple of months, I should think.'

CHAPTER FOUR

'MR VALVERDE is waiting,' Fisher informed Dixie with suppressed urgency.

Tears welling up in her eyes, Dixie settled Spike into his basket.

'Cook's going to bring Spike into the kitchen every day. He doesn't mind her,' the older man told her kindly. 'We'll spoil him rotten if he lets us.'

Nodding, because she didn't trust herself to speak, Dixie focused on the aquarium sitting on the chest. César the fish was at one end, his new lady companion, Milly, at the other. Neither seemed to venture into the other's territory. A bit like her and César Valverde, she conceded ruefully. She lived in his house but saw him only by rare and reluctant invitation.

'I'll take the aquarium down to the kitchen too,' Fisher promised.

'I talk to them every day.'

'Cook could talk the hindleg off a donkey.'

César was pacing the front hall. Lean, mean and magnificent in a lightweight charcoal-grey suit, burgundy shirt and silver grey silk tie, he

surveyed Dixie with glittering dark eyes of enquiry.

'I've kept you waiting…I'm sorry.'

As his attention lingered on her, Dixie
smoothed an uneasy hand down over the skirt of
her chic green summer dress.

César fixedly studied the ragged, uneven hem
of the garment from which several stray threads
still hung. 'What have you done to that dress?'
he demanded.

Dixie had hoped he wouldn't notice. 'After
what you said last night, I thought it might be a
bit too short too…so I let the hem down, but it
didn't go down the way I thought it would—'

'So why didn't you wear something else?'

'Fisher had already taken away my case.'

In thunderous silence, César gritted his even
white teeth. Crossing the hall, he proceeded to
hunker down and pluck away the hanging threads
with impatient fingers.

'You see, I needed something to occupy me
last night. Scott's been sent to New York for a
while…I didn't even get to say goodbye…' Her
voice trailed away as she absently watched a
shard of sunlight glance over César's gleaming
blue-black hair and then marvelled at the incredible length of his inky black lashes as she gazed
down at him.

'Life's little cruelties toughen one up,' César advised with an outstanding lack of sympathy as he vaulted back upright. He pressed her towards the front door. 'And now, while you're in Spain, you won't have the distraction of thinking of Scott being back here in London.'

'I guess not…and it's a great opportunity for him.' Dixie gave a determined smile. 'Scott's boss must think very highly of him to offer him such a chance.'

César turned to her once inside the limo. 'You have blue shadow on one eyelid and green on the other.'

'Is it noticeable?'

'It's screaming at me.'

Dixie nodded, dug a tissue out of her bag and removed the shadow without resorting to a mirror. She then dug out a paperback and proceeded to read. This obvious solution to coping with César, who would sooner she was seen but not heard, had occurred to her the night before. If she dug her nose into a book he wouldn't feel he had to talk to her, and she wouldn't find herself inadvertently trying to chat to him.

An hour and a half later she hurried up the steps of his private jet, her excitement unconcealed. 'I've never been on a plane before,' she told the flight attendant without hesitation. 'I've never been abroad before either!'

'Sit down and behave like a grown-up,' César growled in her ear from behind.

Reddening, Dixie dropped down into the nearest seat.

'You sit with me.' César had the embattled air of·a male restraining his temper with the greatest of difficulty.

Dixie wondered what she had done wrong. She hadn't spoken to him once, not once, and she'd assumed he would be delighted to be able to forget her existence. She'd had a great chat with his chauffeur on the way through the airport, and then there had been that lovely old lady she'd got talking to in the VIP lounge. Yet far from appreciating the space and privacy she had awarded his natural reserve, César had become tenser and colder by the minute.

As the jet taxied down the runway, Dixie started getting nervous at the prospect of her first take-off. In an effort to distract herself, she turned to look at César, where he sat to her right, a file open in one lean hand. 'What did I do that annoyed you?'

His hard profile clenched. He looked at her broodingly, shimmering dark eyes glinting from below semi-lowered lids. 'You're everybody's best friend. You have no dignity, no normal reticence. You told my chauffeur about Scott—'

'He told me about his daughter's marriage breaking up.'

'That's the point. He's an employee. I didn't even know he *had* a daughter!' César condemned as the engines whined and the jet began to race down the runway.

Dixie turned a whiter shade of pale and clutched at the arms of her seat with protruding knuckles. 'Oh, golly, I feel sick... I'm scared...this is really frightening... I don't think I want to fly *anywhere*!' she suddenly wailed, jerking loose her seatbelt and starting to rise.

She was tugged back safely into her seat by a restraining hand. As she attempted to catch her breath, César took one look at the sheer panic etched on her face and, meshing lean fingers into her hair, held her fast and kissed her.

Dixie forgot she was on board a jet. She forgot she was afraid. She even forgot to be afraid of *him*. In shock, she felt the hard male heat of his mouth prying apart her lips. Like lightning suddenly unleashed inside her, that kiss zapped out every sane thought and burned her up with excitement. Without realising it, she clutched at him. As the tip of his tongue expertly invaded the moist sweetness of her mouth she shuddered, as if she was in a force ten gale, and pushed the fingers of one hand ecstatically into the springy silk of his hair.

He felt so good she wanted to sink into him and lose herself for ever in the frantically seductive tide of physical sensation assailing her. She was wildly, madly aware of every throbbing cell in her own body. Fierce energy and urgency was penned up inside her, fighting for release. She never passed the point of temptation. She got one taste of temptation and simply succumbed.

Without warning, César jerked away, long fingers dropping to her forearms to set her back from him. Dixie opened her eyes, blinked, and focused on his lean strong face, the feverish glitter in his brilliant dark incisive eyes. She couldn't see his anger, yet somehow she could *feel* his anger, silently striking out at her in the unbearably tense atmosphere.

'Did I do that wrong as well?' she asked, struggling to come to grips with the devastating reality that César Valverde had actually kissed her.

His incredible lashes dropped down over his eyes. He released her, but the silence continued to seethe.

'Of course you only did it because I started to panic about flying.' Dixie twisted her head away and tried to stop shivering.

'Even Jasper is likely to expect an engaged couple to exchange the occasional kiss,' César imparted very flatly.

Dixie swallowed hard on that assurance. She would have thought Jasper would be shocked rigid if they exchanged a passionate kiss in front of him. *Passionate?* No, not for César, she decided, her tummy muscles tightening with sudden extreme discomfiture. For César it had obviously just been a casual kiss, something in the nature of a reluctant rehearsal. He was probably affronted that she had thrown herself into that kiss as if they were Romeo and Juliet.

'You think I enjoyed you kissing me too much.' Looking anywhere but at him, Dixie was extremely embarrassed but determined to clear the air. 'You took me by surprise… I guess with your experience you're used to that kind of overboard response, but it was more of an experiment for me—'

'I think this may well be one of those deep conversations better shelved.'

Unexpectedly, Dixie turned back to face him, a sunny smile of anticipation slowly curving her reddened mouth. 'You don't understand. If *you* can make me feel like that, I can hardly wait to find out how Scott can make me feel!'

The silence refused to break. Indeed, the silence sat there like a huge brick wall barrier.

César stared steadily back at her, dark eyes black as a stormy night, not a revealing muscle moving on his strong dark features.

As the tension crackled sky-high, Dixie frowned in bewilderment. 'I just wanted to re-assure you that I wasn't being silly and feeling attracted to you or anything like that... I mean I just *couldn't* be attracted to you...you're so...' She faltered to a halt in the pin-dropping quiet greeting that impulsive explanation.

'So...*what*?' César invited, with the most le-thally intimidating smile.

Dixie gulped, an odd, thrilling chill running down her taut spine, as if she was dicing with death on the edge of a precipice. 'So...so far removed from me—'

'That's not what you were about to say.'

'I was getting too personal again,' Dixie back-tracked in haste.

'*So what*, Dixie?'

Mesmerised by the full onslaught of his dark stare, she whispered, 'So cold, so self-absorbed, so inhuman...'

'And you are so refreshingly, dangerously... honest,' César murmured.

Dixie had stopped breathing without under-standing why. Then at that moment the bright voice of the flight attendant broke the spell. 'The captain wondered if Miss Robinson would like to visit the flight deck, sir.'

César rested his arrogant dark head back. 'I should think Miss Robinson would be delighted.

Don't touch anything, Dixie...don't fall against anything either.'

The flight attendant giggled.

Dixie went pink as she rose from her seat, well aware that César hadn't been joking.

By the time Dixie got out of the jet at Malaga, her cheerful outlook had vanished. Reality had dug in and dug in hard.

Until now she had cravenly avoided thinking about the masquerade that loomed at journey's end. She had concentrated her thoughts on simply spending time with Jasper again. That was in itself a most pleasurable prospect. She was intensely fond of Jasper and refused to dwell on the idea that he might be seriously ill. What could not be cured had to be endured. Dixie had learnt that lesson at an early age.

Only now, as she wandered in César's purposeful wake through the airport, was she becoming miserably, guiltily aware that she was about to take part in a deception which went against every principle she had been raised to respect. She had been in the depths of despair when César had approached her with his proposition. Sick with worry about Petra's debts, and exhausted by the strain of working two jobs, she had been further devastated to learn of Jasper's failing health...

And she remembered sitting in César's Ferrari later that same evening, listening against her will to his silver-tongued assurance that their pretend engagement would be the best news Jasper had ever heard. César had made it all sound so simple, so harmless. He had even made her feel that to refuse would be selfish and cruel.

But the imminent prospect of lying to an old man as sincere and trusting as Jasper made Dixie feel sick with nerves and guilt. She stumbled round a baggage trolley and stood gazing into space. How could she look Jasper in the face and lie?

'*Dixie!*' Striding back to intercept her for about the fourth time, César snapped an imprisoning hand over her shoulder to turn her in the right direction again. '*Accidenti!* Didn't you even notice you'd lost me?'

'No...'

Outside, César pressed her into a chauffeured limo with the driven aspect of a male who had valiantly herded an entire flock of wandering and wilful sheep through the crowded airport.

Dixie emerged from her uneasy thoughts to find César doing up her seatbelt. Jawline hard as a rock, he tightened it the way a medieval jailer might have tightened a chain on a prisoner likely to try and escape. 'Now just stay there...don't move.'

Lashes fluttering, Dixie gazed up at his lean, dark, devastatingly attractive face in total bemusement. 'Where would I move to?'

'And you can ditch that miserable expression. Agonising over Scott is forbidden!' Grim dark eyes scanned her startled face without remorse. 'You have a part to play, and although I don't expect your performance to qualify for an Oscar, I *do* expect you to look reasonably happy.'

'But I wasn't agonising over Scott. If you must know, I was worrying about lying to Jasper—'

'Leave the lying to me.'

'Yes, you'll be so much better at that than I could ever be,' Dixie conceded reflectively.

Flames of gold flared in César's incredulous gaze. 'I don't know how I've got you this far without strangling you,' he confessed in a shaken undertone. 'I have reserves of restraint I never knew I had.'

Dixie snatched in a stricken breath. 'That's a horrible thing to say…what could I possibly have done to deserve that?'

César spread the fingers of his two clenched brown hands very slowly. 'You want to know…you *really* want to know?'

He was truly angry, Dixie realised in shock and perturbation, violet eyes very wide.

'One…' César gritted, like a male about to embark on a very long speech. 'You have the attention span of a flea. Two…you wandered through the airport like a headless chicken. Three…you're still acting like the office junior. Exactly when are you planning to psych yourself into the role of my fiancée? While you were giggling like a schoolgirl with my cabin staff and trying on their hats, I heard you refer to me three times as *Mr* Valverde. Four…you're emotionally manic—'

'M-manic?' Dixie parroted tremulously.

'Either you're acting euphoric or you're on the brink of tears! There is no happy medium, no nice quiet level of normality.'

'My life hasn't *been* very normal recently,' Dixie pointed out, her throat thickening.

'Point five,' César growled rather raggedly as her violet eyes shimmered in helpless reproach, 'I do not like being ignored.'

Like a spoilt child, convinced that the entire world revolved around him, was Dixie's first thought. Fortunately she didn't say it out loud, but she was tempted to remark that she didn't recall him showing any sign that he wished to speak to her himself. Surely he didn't expect her to sit beside him in total silence, like a glove puppet waiting for an empowering hand?

'I wasn't ignoring you. I thought you preferred me to keep a low profile—'

'A *low* profile?' César echoed in a tone of rampant disbelief.

Dixie reddened and clasped her hands tightly together on her lap. 'You have so many hang-ups—'

'Hang-ups?' César ejaculated rawly.

'You're not a people person. And just having fun is beneath you. That brain of yours just never stops ticking and dissecting things…you are so deadly serious all the time. It's unnerving.'

'I find you equally unnerving,' César imparted after a staggered pause.

Involuntarily, Dixie collided with eyes that were silvered by a stray shard of sunlight filtering into the car, eyes that were dazzlingly beautiful in that lean, dark, brooding face, and her heart jumped and her tummy twisted and her conscience smote her all at once. In confusion she turned her head away, but in her mind's eye she was now seeing the unhappy, far too bright and knowing little boy whom Jasper had once sadly described to her. A cynic at the age of five, with a deep distrust of adults.

A wealthy young mother's fashion accessory only while he was still at the cute baby stage, César had been the pretty much unwelcome result of an impulsive and short-lived marriage. His parents had parted before he was even born. His playboy father had wanted his estranged wife to terminate her pregnancy, and when she'd failed to follow his advice had considered himself absolved of any further responsibility, other than financial, towards his son.

Finding a toddler's needs more of a nuisance than she had envisaged, César's youthful mother, Magdalena, had regularly left him with an ever-changing succession of nannies for weeks on end. As soon as she could she had put César into an English boarding school, and had often found it more convenient to simply leave him there during the long vacations.

'Magdalena was very immature. Her own parents were dead, so she had no support. She often had good intentions but she was hopelessly selfish,' Jasper had explained heavily. 'Forever promising to visit César at school but always letting him down. One of his stepfathers encouraged her to make more effort for a while, but he was soon out of the picture again.'

So it was no wonder that César was a complete loner, Dixie conceded tautly, already deeply regretting her censure. She had been unjust and unkind. César couldn't help being the way he was. By the time Jasper had got hold of him, at twelve, the damage had been done. César had walled up his emotions. He had never had a real home, never had a proper family or even siblings to tease him, never been loved just for him-self...except by Jasper.

'Why are you looking at me like that?' César demanded in sheer frustration as the limo drew up at a private airstrip where a helicopter awaited them.

Shaking her head in mingled emotion and em-barrassment, Dixie made no response. But she had suddenly appreciated that César might talk about Jasper in that cool, offhand way of his, but that Jasper Dysart was probably just about the only person in the whole world whom César ac-tually cared about.

And if anything happened to Jasper, César was in all probability going to be absolutely devas-tated. Jasper was César's one weakness. And suddenly the extravagant lengths César was pre-pared to go to in his determination to make Jasper happy struck Dixie as the most touching, telling thing ever...and the tears welled up.

'OK...' Tensing, César raised expressive lean brown hands in an attempted soothing motion that did not come naturally to him. 'You don't fancy the helicopter, but the alternative is hours of driving through the mountains and spending the night in a hotel.'

Dixie tore her shimmering gaze from César and said chokily, 'Actually I was thinking about you.'

'Don't think about me. I really do not *want* you thinking about me.'

Dixie nodded jerkily.

César reached for her knotted fingers, straightened them out and threaded on the opulent diamond engagement ring.

'I'll do the best I can to convince Jasper...I promise!' Dixie swore feverishly. 'I'll act just the way he would expect me to act if I was in love.'

'What's that likely to entail? No, no, make it a surprise,' César advised as he edged her by subtle motions out of the car.

'I'll try to think of you the way I think of Scott...' Dixie confided very seriously.

'That could be dangerous. You might fall in love with me instead.'

Dixie sent him an arrested look full of such astonishment that César stared back at her, hard black eyes narrowing and glinting, fabulous bone structure tautening. Quickly her mind went empty, and it was suddenly so hard to breathe, so impossible to look away.

Abruptly, César removed his intense gaze from her. 'I may be a cold bastard, but I don't want this charade to cause any lasting damage. A woman who cries her heart out over a cannibalised goldfish has to be more than usually vulnerable. In fact when I saw you leaning over that fountain asking the survivor how he could have stooped to eating his only friend, I decided you were totally off this planet.'

'I get very fond of my pets, but there is no danger that I would *ever* get fond of you!' Dixie retorted in fierce self-defence, and she scrambled into the helicopter without a backward glance.

For the duration of the flight over the snow-capped sierras of Andalusia, Dixie was deep in her own thoughts. She was reliving that whirling other-worldly sensation that overwhelmed her whenever she met César Valverde's eyes. It was terrifying, embarrassing, and yet weirdly thrilling. And she had finally worked out what was the matter with her…

César was gorgeous. Undoubtedly she was re-acting to his intense sexual charisma. It was not that she was mentally attracted to him, she reasoned, it was that she was *bodily* attracted to him. Like when she was peckish and the vision of a tempting dessert formed inside her head. Foolish, harmless and meaningless, she told herself, resolving to keep a tighter rein on herself now that she understood the problem. And putting César on a level with chocolate fudge cake made her feel a lot less threatened and self-conscious. She would soon get over such silliness.

When the helicopter began to descend, it was dusk. As the craft tilted, Dixie gazed down into a thickly wooded hidden valley, a silvered road snaking like a ribbon through it into the distance. A beautiful hacienda clung to the steep forested slopes. The seemingly endless stretch of pale walls and red-tiled roof glimmered in the fading light. The helicopter set down on a helipad within the perimeter walls.

César sprang out and stretched in a hand to assist her. Dixie grasped his fingers, her eyes brimming with surprise. '*This*…is where Jasper lives?'

'What did you expect? A little cottage complete with butterfly net in the foothills?'

Dumbly, Dixie shook her head. It was a simply huge house, with all the elegant opulence that only the very, very rich take for granted. As they crossed an exquisitely landscaped courtyard, with a softly playing fountain to the side entrance, César reached down and closed his hand over hers. 'Let's get the big announcement over with.'

A smiling middle-aged woman awaited them in the vast tiled hall. As she spoke, a frown instantly indented César's brow.

'What's wrong?'

'Jasper's not here.' César dropped her hand again—there now being no necessity to pretend he wanted even that small amount of physical contact with her, Dixie assumed. 'His housekeeper hasn't a clue where he is either. Typical

Jasper! And in his state of health what on earth is he doing running about the countryside?'

'Maybe you should have phoned him to tell him we were coming.'

'I wanted to surprise him.' César sent her an impatient glance. 'Out of character for me, but exactly the kind of impractical impulse that Jasper would expect from a newly engaged couple!'

Dixie stared at him, not quite grasping the connection.

César's wide, sensual mouth twisted. 'I thought the very sight of me arriving with you unannounced would make us look more convincing...like I couldn't wait to show you off!' he pointed out in exasperation as he strode back to address the hovering housekeeper in fluent Spanish again. 'Ermina will show you up to my room. I'll need to make some calls to run Jasper to earth!'

An older man laden with their luggage was already heading up the ornate wrought-iron and stone staircase. Dixie followed the housekeeper up to the first landing, briefly stilling with an uncertain frown. She flushed. No, she must have misheard him. César couldn't have said '*my* room'. He couldn't possibly be expecting her to share his bedroom!

But minutes later Ermina showed her into a very large and luxuriously furnished bedroom, where her luggage and César's sat together like a statement. Dixie surveyed the bed, with its massive intricately carved headboard. It was an extremely big bed. No, she was being ridiculous. This was some silly misunderstanding. After all, Jasper was very old-fashioned, and rather fond of muttering about the appallingly lax moral habits of modern youth.

Tilting her chin and striving to suppress her discomfiture, Dixie went downstairs again to find César. She located him in a magnificent library, and for a split second her awed and eager appraisal of all those tempting shelves of books made her still in wonderment.

César was on the phone, talking in Spanish. His dark, deep drawl sounded so…so sexy, Dixie reflected dimly, listening to all those fluid rolling vowels with instinctive appreciation, a curious little quiver fingering down her spine. She studied him. Even after hours of travelling, César retained his incredible elegance, and he paced the room with the prowling sure-footed grace of a leopard.

Turning his arrogant dark heard, César finally chose to acknowledge her presence in the doorway. 'If you're hungry, Ermina will fix you some supper.'

It was her cue to depart again. Staying put took courage.

'There's been a bit of a mix-up.' Dixie shuffled her feet restively. 'They've gone and put my stuff in with yours...in the same room, I mean, and I don't have the Spanish to explain that...well, you know—'

'No, I don't know.' César elevated one satiric black brow with daunting cool. 'Naturally we have to share a bedroom. Jasper's not an idiot. If we slept apart he would never believe this engagement was for real!'

CHAPTER FIVE

OPEN-MOUTHED, Dixie stared back at César, heated colour rising in a slow tide beneath her pale skin. 'You really expect me to share your room?' she whispered in disbelief.

César cast aside the cordless phone. 'Where are you coming from on this? Clarify the problem for me.'

The weighted silence pulsed.

Recognising the chill hardening his brooding dark features, Dixie drew in a sustaining breath. 'I couldn't possibly sleep in the same bed. I didn't bargain on anything like that when I agreed to this arrangement.'

'Didn't you? You sold your immediate future to me for a price. I've paid that price. You were up to your throat in debt, and scared witless of being dragged into court to answer for your dishonesty. You are not in a position to call the shots here,' César warned with icy bite, studying her as if she had crawled out from beneath a piece of furniture and was in dire need of being thoroughly squashed. 'And you are *far* from being the little innocent you like to pose as for Jasper's benefit!'

That full frontal attack came at Dixie out of nowhere and she was quite unprepared for it. She gaped at him. 'I'm not dishonest, and—'

'You *are* dishonest. You ran up debts you hadn't a prayer of paying. You are no better than a thief.' César's eloquent mouth curled with contempt. 'You should've faced up to that by now. And when you start trying to pretend to be something you're not with me as well, it's time to call a halt to your fantasies!'

'Fantasies…?' Dixie repeated weakly.

'The big parties? The ludicrously expensive trappings for a rented apartment? What else but fantasies? Maybe you were trying to buy friends. But I don't have the slightest pity for you,' César informed her without hesitation. 'I know you have a brain, and I *know* you had to know exactly what you were doing—'

'But those parties weren't mine…and neither was the apartment!' Dixie broke in helplessly.

'I think you assumed that Jasper might pick up the bills for you. What a shock it must've been to learn that Jasper is as poor as a church mouse!' Brilliant dark eyes like lasers probed her shattered expression for a betraying response. 'Did you really think I wouldn't work that possibility out?'

Pale as milk and trembling, Dixie was appalled by his suspicions. 'I honestly don't know what you're talking about, and if you'd let me explain about those debts in the first place, you'd have known that—'

'You worked your way into Jasper's soft heart and stupidly assumed he was loaded?' César incised with stinging scorn. 'I'm not a fool. First the friendship, next the extravagant spending spree, and then no doubt you wrote to Jasper, anxiously confiding that you had got into some financial hot water—'

'No…no, that's crazy!' Dixie was falling into deeper shock by the second.

'And then possibly Jasper wrote back saying how much he would've liked to be able to help you…but unfortunately, since his trust fund was embezzled by a crooked accountant over ten years ago, he has been wholly dependent on me!'

'I wouldn't *do* anything like that…wouldn't have dreamt of worrying Jasper with my problems!' Dixie's eyes were stricken as she moved her head in a negative motion. 'You have such a hateful opinion of other human beings, César. You're always looking for the bad, never, ever the good.'

Unimpressed by that pained condemnation, César continued to survey her from his towering height, eyes as cold as black ice. 'Oh, I acquit you of real evil, but I'm certain that at some stage you must've attempted to fish yourself out of trouble by approaching Jasper for a loan.'

'Then perhaps you ought to ask him for my letters,' Dixie countered with as much dignity as she could muster. She lifted her head high, her mouth tightly compressed with the effort self-control demanded of her. 'And perhaps you ought to get your facts right too.'

'And where could I possibly have got them wrong?' César traded very drily.

'My sister threw those parties—'

'You don't have a sister. You don't have a single living relative.'

'I'm talking about my *step*sister, Petra Sinclair. She's made quite a name for herself as a model. The apartment was hers. When I first came to London I lived with her, and because she was away so much she opened this bank account so that I could settle her bills. Then everything went wrong… *somehow*!' Dixie shook her aching head again, her forehead furrowing, as if she was still trying to come to grips with how everything had gone so very wrong.

'Petra…*Sinclair*?' César queried, with the oddest stress and a look of surprise.

While sensing something not quite right, either in his intonation or in his narrowed stare and hardening jawline, Dixie was far too involved in telling her story to let his curious reaction to her sister's name register with her for more than a second.

'Petra decided to go to Los Angeles and become an actress, and she's still over there...I don't know where. Well, you see, the deputy bank manager...who was just incredibly *nice*,' Dixie stressed, and then fell into a somewhat erratic explanation about the joint account and the way she had often ordered goods and services on Petra's behalf.

'If you're telling me the truth, Leticia Zane would've been well aware that *Petra* was her client.'

'Of course she was,' Dixie confirmed wearily. 'But once Miss Zane realised that Petra had left the UK she was furious. I don't think she believed me when I told her that I didn't have an address for Petra—'

'Probably not. I can check all this out,' César warned her, but for some reason the warning emerged almost as an afterthought, the suggestion being that he had already decided that she was telling the truth.

'Go ahead. I've got nothing to hide.'

He asked her several more probing questions. The set of his mouth grew more grim. 'I take back what I said about your brain,' he breathed. 'It's weak on survival skills and common sense.'

'You don't understand. Petra was terribly upset about the whole thing too, but by then, with the expense of moving to LA, she was really broke. If you only knew how terrific she was whcn my stepmother was ill—'

'She *was*?' For some reason César sounded very surprised to receive that assurance.

'Petra was absolutely wonderful, and I was very grateful. She really is a great person—a little thoughtless sometimes, but very generous and kind with everything she's got...when she's got it, I mean,' Dixie concluded rather limply.

'Generous...kind,' César echoed, as if he had never heard the words before, his deep, forceful drawl having for some reason sunk to the level of a constrained whisper.

Dixie looked up worriedly, drained by that outpouring.

César was studying her as if she was some strange life-form he had never come across before. An uncharacteristic mix of reluctant fascination and suppressed disbelief mingled in his brooding dark features. 'I imagine you're extremely *fond* of Petra?'

Dixie nodded in confirmation. She wasn't blind to César's incredulity, but, unlike him, she believed in taking people as they were. Petra's faults did not detract from Dixie's affection for her stepsister. Nor had Dixie ever resented the lack of hands-on help she had received during her stepmother's long illness. Petra and her mother had never got on, and Petra could not have coped with that caring role. In contrast, Dixie had loved her stepmother very much, and had wanted to do everything she could to repay the woman who had taken her into her heart as if she were her own child.

César stared steadily down into Dixie's clear blue eyes, opened his mouth and then finally closed it again. Then curiosity seemed to get the better of him, and he breathed, 'For how long did you take care of your stepmother?'

Dixie told him.

César braced a taut hand on the edge of the handsome library table beside him. 'Quite a slice of your life,' he remarked grimly.

'It's not something I'll ever regret.'

César expelled his breath in a slow hiss and glanced away from her. 'Even I can now accept that you would never have tried to coax money out of Jasper,' he conceded heavily. 'I got the wrong idea. I thought you'd been leading some kind of double life. Now I know that what you see is what you get with you...and that is spooky.'

'Spooky?'

'Let's just say that we don't have a great deal in common.' César flashed her a veiled look.

'Only very rarely am I forced to appreciate what I have by a terrifying glimpse of an alternative lifestyle and outlook.'

Recognising that he no longer believed that there was any truth in those dreadful suspicions he had cherished, Dixie sagged with relief.

'I owe you an apology,' César stated grittily.

'It's not important. You were sure to come up with a really nasty scenario. You can't help the way your mind works,' Dixie said forgivingly. 'Have you had any luck finding Jasper?'

'No...for all I know he's out camping somewhere under the stars!' César's profile tautened with a concern he couldn't hide.

Dixie cleared her throat awkwardly, deciding that now that César was more approachable she should return to the prickly question of sharing a bedroom. 'César, I really do think Jasper would take a very dim view of coming back home to find us in the same bedroom—'

'Don't be ridiculous,' César countered with careless cool. 'We're not living half a century ago.'

'Jasper has very strong Christian beliefs,' Dixie pointed out very gently, conscious that César was sure to believe that he knew best where his godfather was concerned. 'He lives very much in his own little world, and it dates back more than half a century. I honestly believe he would be very shocked and offended at us sharing a room under this roof.'

César dealt her an impatient frown. 'You haven't a clue what you're talking about. Jasper has never questioned what I do in my private life.'

Did you bring your private life into his home? she badly wanted to ask, but couldn't bring herself to that controversial brink. César's notoriety as a ruthless womaniser was a source of very genuine concern and mortification to Jasper. But possibly Jasper had never dared to admit that to César. Indeed, it was hard to picture Jasper standing up to César, of whom he stood in considerable awe.

César swept up the phone again, indicating that the subject was closed.

'César...I'm just not comfortable with this bedroom arrangement,' Dixie persisted valiantly, her mind boggling at the prospect of sleeping in the same room as César, never mind the same bed.

'Quit while you're ahead, Dixie. Allow me to know my own godfather better than you do. Act like I'm Scott,' César suggested with a satiric glance of finality as he strode out of the library.

Dixie made a beeline for the books. An hour later, she climbed upstairs with a towering pile of rather dusty hardbacks, it having proved impossible for her to make a smaller selection. Her cases had already been unpacked for her. Eager to get to bed now that she had her books, she went back downstairs, found the kitchen and helped herself to a glass of milk. Then, back in the bedroom, she located one of the ridiculously glamorous new nighties she had been endowed with and hurried into the beautifully appointed bathroom with its fleecy towels. Stripping off on the spot, she got under the shower.

She was far too strait-laced, she told herself then. César would never dream of making a pass at her! They would each sleep on their own side of what was admittedly a very generously sized bed. There was an adjoining dressing room and with a little mutual care and consideration it needn't be that embarrassing an exercise.

Five minutes after reaching that seemingly sensible conclusion, Dixie was tucked up in bed in the enthusiastic hold of a weighty tome on eighteenth-century philosophy, her shapely figure fetchingly sheathed in palest green silk. When César walked through the bedroom door she was mental miles away, and she didn't hear him.

So when she groped out blindly for her milk, and then was forced to tear her attention from her book and actually look for the glass, she was quite transfixed to suddenly notice César casually peeling off his shirt about ten feet away.

She took in that magnificent expanse of golden brown male flesh and flexing muscles and just gaped.

'Ignore me,' César drawled with supreme casualness, a strange silvered challenge in his dazzlingly bright eyes, his expressive mouth twisting.

Barely breathing, Dixie ducked her head down again, heartbeat racing, mouth dry. The printed page swam. She could see nothing but César, could hear nothing but the rushing in her own eardrums and, preternaturally loud, the soft rasp of a trouser zip. He does this all the time, a dry little voice said inside her head. He's used to sharing a bedroom, a bed. Don't embarrass yourself by reacting in any way. She could breathe if she tried, *couldn't she*? Well, possibly, if she cleared her disobedient brain of wanton images of César Valverde completely unclothed.

Warmth like heated honey pooled in the pit of Dixie's stomach and made her quiver. She wanted to watch him undress. That awareness shook her rigid, but it still took real physical restraint not to lift her head again and peek.

When the bathroom door closed behind César, she drank in oxygen in great needy gulps, her face hot as hellfire with shame. Was this what sexual curiosity felt like? She couldn't ever remember being tempted to spy on Scott. Thank heaven, she thought, genuinely loathing the secret burn of guilty excitement which César's mere presence now unleashed in her. Continued exposure to César's deeply unsettling aura of raw animal sex appeal had finally decimated her natural defences.

César strolled back out of the bathroom. Without the will to stop herself, Dixie peered surreptitiously out from behind her book, glimpsed long powerful thighs lightly dusted with dark curling hair, what might have been the hem of a pair of black silk boxer shorts, and felt as if she was about to have a heart attack.

'I see you hit the library hard.' With easy grace, César swept up a book and glanced through it.

In studious silence, Dixie nodded without looking at him. She didn't trust herself to look at him any more. She was really ashamed of herself. Out of the corner of her eye, she saw him pull back the sheet and slide into bed.

'To think I assumed you would cover yourself from head to toe to share this bed with me,' César confided, in a low-pitched murmur that was terrifyingly intimate.

Her tension shooting up to megawatt heights, Dixie slowly turned her head to register shimmering dark eyes lingering on the ripe curves cradled by sheer silk. A heady surge of colour blossoming in her cheeks, Dixie pressed her book against the swell of her full and now tingling breasts. 'I never thought—'

'There's too many things you never think about...' César mused in a thickened undertone that growled through the beating silence like a warning.

Already fiercely preoccupied with the mortifying throb of her tightening nipples, Dixie was striving to sink herself beneath the more decent concealment of the sheet that had fallen to her waist. Yet colliding head-on with silvered eyes as mesmerically bright as stars in that lean, dark face, she stilled, paralysed by the sudden greedy burst of excitement flaming through her disobedient body.

'Whereas *I* never stop thinking, except in bed, where other more natural instincts take over,' César imparted in a whisper as rich as thick velvet. 'So cold, so inhuman, but *not* in the bedroom, *cara.*'

Dixie found herself leaning over him slightly without even recalling the move that had sent her into that dangerous and inexplicable change of direction. It was like being drawn by a force stronger than she was, to the heart of a fire that might burn but still blazed a cruel attraction for her. 'César...?' she queried shakily, her tongue cleaving to the roof of her dry mouth.

In an almost involuntary motion César lifted a lean brown hand, hard colour accentuating the feverishly taut slant of his high cheekbones. And still Dixie was held there by those stunning silver eyes, fighting to get a grip on a mind that had shut down even as César dropped his hand again, clenching his long fingers into a fist in the humming, dragging quiet. Her soft pink mouth opened, the tip of her tongue creeping out to moisten her generous lower lip.

And with a sudden, driven groan of surrender, César reached for her with two powerfully impatient hands and dragged her down hungrily into his arms. Lightning struck between one second and the next. One moment Dixie was hung on the agonising brink of a craving she did not even fully comprehend, and the next she was lost without hope of recovery.

Her whole body exulted in the ferociously hard demand of César's sensual mouth crashing down on hers. Anything softer would have been cruel disappointment. As he rolled over and pinned her beneath his weight, his tongue stabbing into her mouth to plunder the sweetness within, she was overwhelmed by the rawness of his passion and the shockingly aggressive surge of emotion rising within herself.

Her wondering fingers glossed over his broad, smooth shoulders and then speared convulsively into his luxuriant black hair, to curve to his skull and imprison him. Welded to every sleek muscle in César's big powerful frame, she felt the hot hard thrust of his all-male arousal against her quivering stomach. The responsive heat that burned up inside her reduced her to a mindless jelly.

'Why does this feel so incredibly good?' César ground out accusingly against her reddened lips as they fought in concert to get breath back into their lungs.

César was holding Dixie so tightly that breathing remained more of a challenge than a likely possibility. Hazily studying her own fingers, which were now possessively welded to his cheekbones, Dixie parroted weakly, *'Good?'*

One hand meshed into her thick silky hair, César gazed down at her, brilliant eyes lambent silver pools of fierce frustration. 'This is not the time to think of me as a trial run for Scott—'

'Scott?'

As if he couldn't concentrate long enough to listen, César let one questing hand smooth down over the swell of one full breast. As every skin cell in her shivering body jumped in electrifying reaction, any hope of sanity reasserting itself was quickly lost. Dixie gasped out loud, eyes dilating, head tipping back to expose her throat as she trembled with a hunger as fierce as it was ungovernable.

César breathed something rough and fractured in Italian, his entire attention melded to his own hands as he lifted them to her slight shoulders to brush down the straps that concealed her from his almost reverent gaze. A husky, sexy hiss that was almost agonised escaped him.

'You are *so* gorgeous...' he gritted not quite evenly as the glistening sheer fabric slid down the proud upper slope of her full breasts, catching on prominent pink buds already swollen with excitement.

And in the same self-conscious moment that Dixie tried to cover her wanton flesh, César touched her where she had never been touched before, and the entire world vanished in the violent surge of her own overpowering response. 'César...' she moaned.

'*Madre di Dio....*' César husked, with the self-absorption of a male wholly bent on seduction.

He shaped her tender flesh, his thumbs glancing over the sensitised rosy peaks, making her jerk and squirm helplessly. And then he bent his dark head to a straining pink bud and laved it with his tongue, with the kind of sensational expertise that sent her temperature rocketing to fever-point and wrung strangled sounds from low in her throat.

Her back arched, a tight maddening ache spiralling up between her thighs, sending every inch of her mad with uncontrollable desire. Shuddering in the circle of her arms, César closed his hungry mouth over hers again. She didn't hear the door opening, wasn't aware of anything before Jasper's well-bred voice, raised in a tone of delighted surprise and welcome, interrupted them. 'My dear boy, *when* did you arrive?'

César jerked his head up and Dixie looked past his shoulder in sudden horror and confusion. Jasper was hovering like a small portly Santa Claus suddenly told that Christmas had been axed. Dixie was too shocked even to be grateful for the fact that César was blocking all but her face from Jasper's aghast look of recognition.

'We'll discuss this downstairs, César,' Jasper announced in a deeply shaken and pained tone of censure as he turned on his heel.

CHAPTER SIX

PARALYSED by Jasper's swift entrance and even swifter exit, and the situation she now found herself in, Dixie studied César, who was still staring at the space Jasper had briefly filled, his bemusement doubtless the result of being addressed as though he was a misbehaving teenage boy.

'Porca miseria!' Suddenly coming back to life, César pulled free of Dixie's loosened hold, thrust back the rumpled sheet and sprang out of bed. 'Jasper looked at me as if he hated me!' he exclaimed with the glancing rawness of shock, pushing a not quite steady hand through his wildly tousled black hair, dark, deep-set eyes full of fracturing emotion.

Frantically engaged in righting the bodice of her nightdress, a sob of distress in her voice, Dixie whispered jaggedly, 'I t-told you Jasper wouldn't approve!'

'I wasn't expecting him to return this late and walk right in on us! This is scarcely how I planned to make our announcement. But when I tell him that we're engaged, he'll calm down,' César forecast with frowning conviction.

Unable to look at him any longer, and wishing she shared his confidence, Dixie rolled over on her stomach and stared at the headboard with strained eyes full of deep regret and shame. What had she been doing with César? What had he been doing with her? Her wretched body ached from the severance of his. Cold little shivers of reaction now rippled through her, but deep down inside herself she was hatefully aware that the physical craving which had reduced her to such a level still lingered on like her worst enemy.

'Jasper chose an opportune moment to interrupt us,' César continued with meaningful cool as he banged through the storage units in the adjoining dressing room, evidently in search of clothes. 'Next time you get into bed with me, cover yourself from head to toe.'

'There won't *be* a next time,' Dixie responded in a chagrined undertone. 'I wasn't expecting anything like that to happen.'

'But now you have reassuring proof that I *am* human. Throw a sexually active male into bed with a scantily clad woman putting out provocative signals...and he'll fall from the path of rectitude so fast your head will spin!' César slashed back with defensive bite.

Dixie rolled over and sat up. 'I wasn't provocative,' she protested in dismay and bewilderment at such a charge. 'I was reading my book…I was minding my own business! You just pounced on me!'

Emerging from the dressing room, only half-way into a shirt, César sent her an incredulous look, eyes splintering a silvered challenge. 'You were *begging* for it!'

'I don't even like you…I wouldn't beg you for anything!' Dixie flung back in increasing turmoil.

'No? Very much against my will and my intelligence, I am sexually attracted to you.' As he made that grudging acknowledgement César slung her a brooding look, his darkly handsome features rigid as stone. 'It's really getting on my nerves, but unlike you I'm prepared to be honest about it…I'm not telling the whole world every hour on the hour how much I'm in love with someone else!'

In a complete daze in the aftermath of that gritty confession, Dixie surveyed César with very wide eyes. He was attracted to her? *Personally* attracted to her? Since when? A rosy blush slowly lit her cheeks. 'You're attracted to me…?' she parroted, suddenly feeling very short of breath.

'It's lust, Dixie…pure naked *lust*.' César stressed in sizzling contradiction. 'A complication we can do without…and do without it we will.'

As his brilliant eyes glittered like ice shards, Dixie was mortified. Bowing her head, she pulled her knees up under the sheet and hugged them. She got the distinction, and the message he had gone out of his way to make. Nature was playing the cruellest kind of joke on them both. The sexual chemistry was there, but nothing else, and César was relieved that Jasper's arrival had concluded their intimacy. Dixie was still feeling too embarrassed to feel relieved. Indeed, she could never recall experiencing such intense emotional turmoil.

Anger, resentment, pain, regret. The extent of her own confusion destroyed her ability to think straight. César had left the room before it occurred to her that she ought to go down to see Jasper as well. One didn't avoid dear friends, no matter how awkward the situation might be. Jasper had been embarrassed, and that was her fault. She shouldn't have allowed César to over-rule her misgivings about sharing a room. And now it was her duty to soothe and reassure along-side César. It was time to act like one half of a couple…

As she hurriedly pulled on a light cotton robe, she thought fiercely about Scott. She knew Scott so well. His faults, his strengths. He might take her for granted, but she knew he genuinely liked and respected her as a friend. Beneath the city slicker image he worked so hard to maintain, Scott was a country boy with a love of home cooking. He was always very even-tempered and cheerful. And she did love him, she really *did*, had known the very first night she met him that he was the man for her. Scott's image finally glimmered into being inside her mind's eye. True, his features were a little blurred, but she let her breath escape with relief.

César was right. She hadn't appreciated his bluntness but he had been right, she told herself urgently as she ran a brush through her hair. Those mindless dislocated-from-planet-earth feelings she got every time she looked at César were sheer lust. And staggeringly beautiful looks and magnetic sex appeal were all César had to recommend him. He was impatient, quick-tempered, manipulative, sarcastic, critical and essentially cold...except in the bedroom.

Satisfied by that summing up, Dixie left the room. Of course, she then acknowledged, César was impatient because he liked everything perfect. And he was sarcastic and critical because he was so much cleverer than most people, and it had to be frantically frustrating always having to wait for others to catch up with his reasoning. Being so very rich and powerful had spoilt him, but he couldn't really be blamed for that either, could he? And if he was cold, well, he had endured the most heartbreakingly loveless child-hood, and he was extremely fond of Jasper—in-deed had seemed positively shattered in receipt of what could only have been a disapproving frown from Jasper…

Hearing the dull murmur of distant voices when she reached the main hall, Dixie followed them and found herself outside an ajar door. She was just about to sound a light knock and an-nounce her presence when she heard Jasper speak in a grim voice she had never heard or even imagined she might hear from so gentle a man.

'So you gave my poor little Dixie a ring to seduce her,' Jasper was saying with harsh dis-taste. 'Here she is, compromising her own most deep-felt beliefs and doubtless innocently trust-ing that you *will* eventually marry her! But I don't share her faith, César.'

'*Dio*, I—'

'You tell me you're engaged to her, but not one word do you say about *loving* her,' Jasper broke in stiffly. 'Nor is there any mention of when this hypothetical wedding is to take place!'

'We've just *become* engaged,' César stressed in a driven undertone, sounding just a little des-perate and equally unlike himself.

'You finally met a woman who wanted no part of your kind of loose living. You couldn't take no for an answer, so you offered her an engagement ring. A couple of months from now, when you've lost interest in Dixie, you'll throw her back out of your life again without any consideration for the damage you've done,' the older man condemned curtly.

'*Accidenti!* You've got completely the wrong idea—'

'I *know* you and I *know* Dixie,' Jasper contradicted heavily. 'I imagine she's hopelessly in love with you—and I should've seen this coming. For months she's been telling me about everything you do in her letters. Why couldn't you have left her alone, César? It will be a long time before I can forgive you for this. Dixie's very dear to me. She's gentle and caring and kind...yet you didn't even have enough respect for her not to embarrass her in this house!'

'Let's sit down and talk this over calmly, Jasper,' César replied fiercely.

Outside the door, Dixie slowly retreated. Shocked and distressed by the bitterness of Jasper's censure, she could not immediately see what she could do to sort out such a ghastly mess. This was not the sort of discussion she could play a part in. Jasper would not speak freely with her present, and César would certainly not welcome her interference. And after what Jasper had witnessed in that bedroom it would be difficult to confess the truth about their fake engagement.

'No, I've already told you how I feel,' Jasper was saying tightly. 'I want you to leave this house right now, César. I'll send your clothes after you. If you're going to break Dixie's heart, get it over with when I'm here to look after her.'

'OK…I'll set a date for the wedding,' César drawled flatly.

'Next year?' Jasper suggested, audibly unimpressed by that offer.

'Next *week*!' César suddenly gritted explosively. 'Dixie and I will get married next week!'

Dixie almost fell over her own feet. In her disbelief, she stared wide-eyed at the door.

Complete silence had fallen between the two men. She imagined Jasper was as shocked by that startling announcement as she was.

'That puts quite a different complexion on matters, doesn't it?' Jasper sighed with perceptible relief. He sounded much more like himself, but very weary and oddly breathless. 'So you do love her, even though you can't show it… Well, can't have everything…couldn't make a better choice than Dixie…'

'What's wrong, Jasper?' César exclaimed with raw abruptness. *'Jasper!'*

Reacting instantly to the current of alarm in César's exclamation, Dixie pushed open the door. Jasper was lying unconscious in a chair, looking terribly small and old and ill.

César was bending over him, frantically trying to revive him.

'Get a doctor!' Dixie urged.

César strode across the room to snatch up the phone. He was ashen pale beneath his bronzed complexion, and his dark eyes were blank with shock. He made the call, but for its duration he watched Jasper with appalled intensity, drawing in a shuddering breath of unconcealed relief when he saw his godfather begin to revive and mutter.

'Eduardo Arribas is a friend...he lives just outside the village,' César imparted as he replaced the phone.

Jasper was still confused and rather dizzy. César wanted to carry him up to bed, where he would be more comfortable, but Dixie thought it was better not to move him before the doctor's arrival, and she sent César to get a glass of water for him instead. She patted Jasper's hand soothingly.

'Heart, you know,' he complained weakly. 'Never passed out before...'

'You're tired...that's all. You should've been in bed hours ago.' Dixie reached for the glass César extended, noticing in some surprise that César couldn't hold it steady because his hand was shaking. She pressed the glass gently to Jasper's lips.

'Glad you're here,' Jasper mumbled. 'Both here... Suppose I'll have to face that wretched operation after all—'

'What operation?' César broke in with a sudden frown.

'I'm a silly old duffer...never liked hospitals,' Jasper muttered. 'Eduardo says I need one of those pacemakers fitted.'

Dr Arribas came very quickly. The two men helped Jasper up to bed, and Dixie then sat with him until he fell asleep, quietly reflecting on what she had overheard outside that room downstairs before Jasper's collapse gave all of them something rather more important to worry about.

César had actually promised to marry her next week! César, usually the most rational and cool of males, had been so shaken by his godfather's angry demand that he should leave that he had made a really crazy promise sooner than explain that the situation was not quite as it might have appeared. But then telling his godfather the truth would have been a considerable challenge after Jasper had seen the two of them sharing the same bed. Had César then admitted that their engagement was a complete fake, Jasper would have been even angrier.

Well, fortunately for César Jasper's state of health would protect César from being expected to keep to that insane undertaking to immediately marry her. Jasper would now be scheduled for surgery as soon as possible, and when he was convalescing no doubt César would confess that their supposed engagement had been a well-meant but foolish pretence. And César would just have to brace himself to explain that nothing whatsoever had really happened in that bedroom. *Nothing*, Dixie stressed for her own benefit. Nothing she need ever think about again, she told herself urgently. A moment's weakness, best forgotten.

When Dixie emerged from Jasper's room, she was surprised to find César waiting outside in the corridor.

'You should've come back in after seeing Dr Arribas out…' Her voice trailed away as she met César's haunted dark eyes and registered the strain which had indented harsh lines between his nose and mouth. 'Did Dr Arribas give you bad news of some kind?' she asked anxiously.

'No,' César said stiltedly, turning his head away, his strong profile clenching hard. 'In fact the prognosis is very good. Jasper may have told me that his heart was failing but I gather that was something of an exaggeration. Apparently he was just very much afraid of the idea of having this pacemaker fitted.'

'I can understand that. He's never had to go into hospital before.'

'When Eduardo first diagnosed his condition last year, Jasper buried his head in the sand and refused to consider surgery. He also told Eduardo that under no account was I to be informed,' César shared in a constrained undertone, digging his balled fists into the pockets of his well-cut trousers and moving restively away from her, a powerful tension etched into the taut set of his wide shoulders. 'Jasper *knew* that I would put pressure on him to have the operation…'

'Of course you would've. It's the only sensible option.' Dixie was bewildered by the depth of emotional reaction which César was visibly struggling to contain and conceal from her.

'He was afraid I would bully him into it,' César breathed with suppressed savagery.

'That faint Jasper had tonight has done the trick for you,' Dixie said consolingly. 'He's accepted now that he needs surgery.'

'But he'd never have had that attack tonight if it hadn't been for me!' César suddenly raked back at her, every syllable of that roughened assurance raw with stark guilt and self-loathing. '*Madre di Dio*…I damn near killed him!'

Really shaken by that outburst, Dixie protested instantly, 'That's not true, César. Dr Arribas himself said that this could've happened at any time—'

'*Accidenti!*' César's striking dark features were set with bitter self-condemnation. 'Don't feed me that sentimental bull! Jasper was extremely upset tonight...I've never seen him that upset about anything! Who caused that needless distress? *Me!* Me and my smartass ideas!' he completed savagely.

Shimmering dark eyes raw with angry pain and regret, César spun on his heel and strode away without another word, leaving Dixie standing with a deeply troubled frown.

She breathed in deep and swallowed hard. Every natural urge prompted her to follow César and reason with him. He was being far too hard on himself. She would never have allowed anyone else to walk away in such a state without trying to offer some comfort. But she forcibly restrained herself from such a move.

César, who let his guard down with nobody, had just let his guard down on a positive flood of self-recrimination. A few hours from now he might well look back on that emotional outburst and despise it as an act of weakness. He would, very probably, be most annoyed that she had witnessed that brief loss of self discipline. He was a very private man. And he didn't like it when she got too personal, wouldn't thank her for her interference, she reflected, pained by that knowledge, suddenly finding herself hating the awareness that she couldn't reach out to César.

César was a perfectionist. He had started out with good intentions, buoyant in his confident belief that their fake engagement would delight Jasper. And then it had all suddenly gone horribly wrong. Jasper had been shocked and upset. Jasper had revealed a very hurtful lack of faith in his godson. César must have been shocked enough by that. He certainly hadn't needed to see Jasper collapse in front of his eyes as well.

She slipped back into Jasper's room and sat by his bed watching him sleep. At about three in the morning, his housekeeper, Ermina, came in, her kindly eyes full of concerned affection as she gazed down at her elderly employer and indicated that she would like to take Dixie's place.

Dixie wandered back to the bedroom she had vacated earlier and found herself pacing the floor while she anxiously wondered where César was. Had he simply moved into one of the guest rooms? In the frame of mind he had been in, Dixie didn't think it very likely that César would simply have gone back to bed.

After a certain amount of hesitation, she left the room again and went downstairs. There was still a light burning in the elegant sitting room where César and Jasper had had their unfortunate confrontation earlier. Dixie opened the door. César was slumped in an armchair. He had been drinking. A half-empty brandy decanter sat on the sofa table beside him, and he still had a glass clasped in one taut-fingered hand. He looked at her with curiously unfocused dark eyes.

'*Dio*…' César slurred with brooding wit. 'It's everybody's best friend!'

Dixie's soft heart still went out to him. She was tempted to tell him that he was his own worst enemy. He just could not cope with what had happened tonight. He was trying to drown the nasty unsettling effect of his own emotional turmoil in alcohol. And, since alcohol was a depressant, it had only made things worse.

'You'll feel much better tomorrow if you get some sleep now.'

'Proper little ray of sunshine aren't you? Tell me, how does it feel to know that you got it right and I got it *all* wrong?'

'Got what right?' she prompted uncertainly.

'You said lies were always wrong. You were right. You said I'd be so much better at lying than you. You were *wrong* about that,' César gritted, thrusting long fingers roughly through his black hair. 'When Jasper confronted me, I completely blew it—'

'His attitude upset you…you weren't prepared for it.'

'He hates my guts now.'

Dixie knelt down by his feet and looked up at him with concerned blue eyes. 'Of course he doesn't. It was a storm in a teacup.'

'A storm in a teacup,' César repeated unevenly, gazing down into her wide eyes and blinking slightly.

'You take everything far too seriously. Jasper was taken aback…the bedroom bit was very unfortunate, and then, instead of reassuring him, I bet you got on your high horse—'

'My high horse…?'

Dixie gently removed the glass from his hold and then linked her fingers with his. 'César…look on the bright side.'

'The bright side?'

'All right, I use a lot of clichés but clichés are often spot-on,' Dixie pointed out as his hand closed round hers. 'Here you are, feeling really miserable—'

'Guilty,' César contradicted harshly.

'But when we came here you thought Jasper was dying. Now you know that he has every hope of making a complete recovery.'

'True…' César frowned, as if he hadn't quite absorbed that message yet.

'He'll probably live until he's at least a hundred,' Dixie added bracingly. 'And staying away from him now has only made you feel worse.'

'The sight of me might have upset him again,' César breathed darkly. 'That's why I kept my distance.'

'There you are again, thinking the very worst. Jasper loves you,' Dixie scolded softly. 'He just isn't as naive as you assumed. Because he was so surprised at the idea of us being engaged, he suspected that—'

'I had dishonourable intentions?' César grimaced.

Dixie slowly stood up and tugged suggestively at César's hand, in the hope of getting him upright.

'What are you doing?'

'You need to go to bed.'

César rose with something less than his usual inbred grace, and swayed ever so slightly. Dixie smiled at him. Shorn of his icy reserve, he had such tremendous humanity. His ridiculously long lashes swept down, closing her out for a split second, and then he looked at her again and gave her an almost boyish smile that made her heart give a violent lurch.

'You're so nice—you make me feel very bad sometimes,' César shared.

Dixie's smile died. 'I irritate you.'

'No…it's more like meeting my conscience face to face. I'm getting used to it.'

Dixie's smile glimmered again as they reached the bedroom door and she opened it. 'Do you feel better now?'

'Not so as you'd notice.'

'You were only trying to make Jasper happy. You had good intentions,' Dixie assured him warmly.

César gazed down at her with those stunning silvered eyes, a curious stillness freezing his facial muscles as if some sudden revelation had struck him. As he studied her with bewildering intensity, Dixie entirely forgot the rest of what she had intended to say. He slowly lifted one lean hand and stroked a long forefinger very, very gently along the generous curve of her mouth. Her heart jumped and her breathing arrested, a trail of fire tingling where he had touched.

'Never trust my intentions,' César husked, the accented words velvet-soft. 'I invariably calculate everything right down to the final full-stop.'

'You probably can't help yourself…'

Dixie found it impossible to concentrate when she looked up into that lean, dark fallen-angel face of his. Instinctively she hovered, without acknowledging either her own fierce reluctance to be parted from him or the fact that César had actually tightened his grip on her hand. Indeed, all of a sudden it was as if the world was standing still, and in the interim every sense magically sharpened. She was incredibly aware of each breath that she drew, of the surging pulse of her own blood through hcr vcins...

'I feel...I feel like I'm tipsy,' she confided.

'Least it's not a ''really creep feeling'' this time...' César muttered almost dazedly as his dark head slowly, steadily lowered to hers.

And she stopped breathing, sanity drowning in his brilliant magnetic gaze. As his mouth found hers, with a sweetness that was almost unbearable, she felt her knees start to give. He caught her up into his arms and cannoned backwards into the door to close it. 'Stay with me...I don't want to be alone tonight,' he confessed raggedly.

And then he kissed her again, hard, hungry, drugging kisses that blew her mind and melted her to liquid honey. He might have spoken again. But every time he tried to stop kissing her Dixie held him fast. The wanting had escaped like a damburst inside her, carrying all before it. So powerful was that need she could not resist it.

With an erotic expertise she was defenceless against, César let his tongue delve deep, emulating a far more intimate possession. Sealed in his arms, she trembled violently, heartbeat racing, pulses thrumming. Bringing her down on the bcd, hc knclt ovei hei, ieleasiиg die tle on her robe, tugging it down out of his path as he pressed his mouth hotly to the sensitive skin at the base of her throat, and she jerked and whimpered out loud.

That betraying sound made César jerk up his head. He gazed down at her then, and stilled, tension snaking through every muscle of his lean, powerful body. 'No, I'm not sober…this shouldn't be happening, *cara*,' he began with breathless urgency. 'I'm not in control.'

'Why should you be?' Dixie asked helplessly.

Disconcerted by that unexpected response, César stared down into her starry eyes, and he dragged his hands from her slender forearms like a male fighting himself every step of the way. A long shudder racked him. 'Stop looking at me like that,' he urged unsteadily.

Dixie was fascinated. 'Like what?'

With a stifled expletive, César closed his eyes and snatched in a jagged breath of restraint. *'Accidenti!'* he groaned. 'I want you so *much*…I've never wanted a woman as desperately as I want you right now!'

That acknowledgement of her feminine power was like a shot of adrenalin in Dixie's veins. It was a power she had never dreamt she might possess. There was no rational thought in the manner in which she reached up to César and found his wide, sensual mouth again for herself.

An intoxicating sense of joy surged up inside her, lending a fevered edge to the fierce pulse-beat of desire thrumming wildly through her.

César reacted to that invitation by flattening her to the bed. As he connected with her shapely curves he growled deep in his throat with all-male pleasure. They exchanged searing, scorching kisses while Dixie tried stubbornly to unbutton his shirt without disconnecting herself from him.

César made one last attempt to get a grip on the situation. 'We *can't*...' Resolution failing as she spread her hands appreciatively over his magnificent torso, he raised her up in his powerful arms and struggled as clumsily as a teenager to extract her from her nightdress, while letting the tip of his tongue dip between her parted lips before he groaned in belated completion, 'Can't do this...'

'Shut up...' Dixie sealed her lips wonderingly to a smooth, hard shoulder. Like an addict, she drank in the scent and the hot salty taste of his bronzed skin. Everything about him felt so good, so right, so perfect. She started to work steadily downwards, in love with every sensation she shared with him, overwhelmed by a glorious sense of freedom.

'Say my name...' César breathed jerkily.

'Cúuur...'

'Again,' he purred, like a big hungry cat, trembling as she reached the flat, taut muscles of his stomach.

'César…César…César,' Dixie sighed voluptuously, engaged in following her every sensual instinct, smoothing exploring fingers down over his long muscular thighs, discovering the distinctly shocking bulge of his pronounced arousal, but only for a split second.

With a broken hiss of impatience, César wrenched at his zip and started kissing her breathless again. Her heart sang; her whole body blazed. As he fought his way out of his clothes he found her breasts, and it became even more of a struggle to undress and make love to her at one and the same time. Dixie had never even imagined such explosive passion could exist, and she revelled in it. She couldn't get close enough to him. He couldn't get close enough to her.

'You were made for me, *cara*…' César closed his mouth reverently to a rosy pink nipple and laved the straining bud with his tongue.

Her spine arched and she panted with helpless pleasure, hands biting into his shoulders. The illusion that she was in control was gone by then, but she didn't care. He dragged her down into a frantic hot well of excitement, where all she could do was feel and react to the incredible intensity of sensation. Her skin felt as if it was burning over her bones, super-sensitive to his every caress, and she just couldn't stay still.

'You meet my passion with your own,' César muttered with intense appreciation. 'You make me burn for you, *cara*.'

He traced the length of a slim trembling thigh, and the throbbing ache at the heart of her suddenly surged to screaming proportions. As he sought out the moist heat of her most sensitive flesh, she flung her head back and writhed. The surging excitement was almost intolerable. Her temperature was rocketing, her body electrified.

'I can't bear it…I can't bear it!' she suddenly gasped wildly.

César crushed her reddened lips under his again and made her bear it, hot, timeless moments of bittersweet pleasure that drove her crazy. And then he shifted over her, sliding between her thighs, pushing up her knees. In her fevered state, she understood only that at last the unbearable ache of emptiness might be satisfied.

'*Dios*… I can't wait any longer,' César growled.

And she opened her eyes and looked up at him, absorbing the feverish flush on his high cheekbones, the silvered intensity of his eyes, the sheer hunger all for her, and it made her feel that she was flying as high and free as a kite.

As he arched over her, the hot, hard surge of his hungry invasion took her by surprise. The sensation was so new to her she froze in astonishment, and then he thrust deeper, and a sharp, piercing pain dragged a startled cry from her lips.

César stilled in bemusement. 'I'm the first...?' he exclaimed, thunderstruck.

As the pain receded she shifted helplessly beneath him, unable to think, not wanting to speak, longing only to luxuriate in the incredibly intimate feel of him inside her. And that one tiny movement of hers destroyed whatever shred of self-control César had gained from his shock at her innocence. With a ragged groan he thrust deeper still, with passionate urgency, no more able than she to detach himself from the driving demands of his own body.

All awareness of self fell away as he engulfed her in his stormy rhythm. Wild and mindless pleasure controlled her. Her heart thundering against her breastbone, she rode that storm with him. All that mattered was that he shouldn't stop, shouldn't deny the remorseless craving he had unleashed within her. And he drove her to a frenzied climax that made her cry out in ecstasy, her body convulsing in what felt like a thousand pieces as he slammed into her one last time.

Afterwards she felt as if she was falling and falling, down into endless layers of soft cotton wool. And although later she would dimly recall César trying to rouse her to speech, she just couldn't stay awake in the hold of the most seductive contented peace she had ever known.

CHAPTER SEVEN

DIXIE woke up only when a maid pulled open the curtains. Blinking sleepily, she began to sit up, only then realising that she was no longer in César's bedroom.

'Lunch will be ready in one hour, *señorita*,' the smiling maid informed her in perfect English. 'Señor Valverde asked me to wake you.'

A Technicolor replay of what she had been doing shortly before dawn with César assailed Dixie. Shock reeled through her in waves. She could not understand how a mere few hours ago making love with César could have seemed so right, so natural and so inevitable.

César had been drinking, far from his usual unemotional and rational self. But even in that state César had attempted to call a halt. In fact he had tried to be the voice of reason more than once, Dixie remembered. With a sinking heart she recalled ripping him out of his shirt. Colour ran like a banner of shame into her cheeks. She had taken advantage of César...

How could she have done that? He had kissed her first, hadn't he? He had started it...but he had also tried to stop it. But she had wanted him, craved him, shamelessly clung. High on the discovery of the power a woman could have over a man, she had discarded every inhibition. Oh, dear heaven, was there the remotest possibility that she could ever look César Valverde in the face again?

As the maid carried in her clothing and proceeded to hang each garment in the built-in wardrobes, Dixie was frozen by ever-deepening panic to the bed. She was picturing César as he had been in the early hours, César as she had never seen him before. César, unusually vulnerable, knocked for six by Jasper's collapse and his own guilty conscience.

In kissing her, he had surrendered to a moment's temptation. And she had entirely misread the situation. César had really just been seeking the reassuring warmth of human contact, but, being César, he had expressed that need in the form of a sexual invitation. What she should have done was give him a hug or talk to him...or something.

It was all *her* fault. How could she blame him? According to the magazines she read, men weren't good at withstanding temptation. The average single male was programmed to say yes every time. No way could César be held accountable for what she had wantonly encouraged him to do!

He had been so shocked when he'd realised that she was still a virgin. Dixie groaned. She had even gone to sleep while César had presumably been trying to talk to her about what they had just done and why they shouldn't have done it! Within five seconds that speed-of-light intelligence of his would have homed in on the fact that he had made a major mistake. Suddenly she was very grateful that César had shifted her out of his room and slotted her into a guest room bed.

Sliding off the bed, she went for a shower. Then she put on an elegant blue skirt and matching sleeveless top. With every passing minute her inner turmoil simply increased.

Why *had* she cast away every principle and just seized César along with the moment? She hadn't thought of Scott once! But then she had never got past friendship with Scott. And clearly she had a more physical nature than she had ever appreciated. That was obviously why she had lost control with César.

Last night's events had upset her equilibrium as well, but she hadn't recognised her own vulnerability. She had succumbed to what César had earlier bluntly described as 'pure naked lust'. She winced at the label, but there it was. César had awakened the sexual side of her nature.

Better to face that mortifying fact head-on rather than make silly sentimental excuses for herself and begin imagining that she was now falling in love with César! Hadn't that stupid thought been in the back of her mind as she'd drifted blissfully off to sleep in his arms? Yes, it had been. Her subconscious already trying to provide a more acceptable excuse for her behaviour.

But she was *not* falling in love with César. She loved Scott...or did she? She was no longer so sure of that fact. From the moment César had come close she had begun thinking less and less about Scott. Suddenly she didn't know what was going on inside her own head any more. But she badly wanted to see Scott again, and reinforce her feelings for him. Loving Scott from afar was safe; loving César would be emotional suicide. How many times had César already warned her not to get too keen on him?

As she sat at the dressing table, feverishly brushing her hair, a light knock sounded on the door.

In the mirror, she saw César's tall dark figure. Paralysis set in instantaneously.

In beautifully cut chinos the colour of toffee and a black polo shirt, César looked drop dead gorgeous. All bronzed and dark and dangerous. Her heart lurched and she quivered in dismay.

'Let's not talk about earlier,' she heard herself say tautly. 'We should forget it ever happened.'

'Dixie, I—'

'Please don't say any more,' Dixie broke in at frantic speed.

'I can't forget it ever happened.' The assurance was harsh.

'Work at it…you'll be surprised. I always think mistakes are forgotten the quickest, but maybe you don't make enough mistakes to know that the way I do,' Dixie muttered rather limply, fiddling with the hairbrush, avoiding even his reflection now, because even his reflection sent her heartbeat crazy. 'How's Jasper?'

'He slept late. I haven't actually seen him yet, but I gather he's fine. It was Ermina who told me he would be coming down to lunch,' César proffered with audible impatience. 'We *have* to talk about this, Dixie. I need to know what you're trying to say to me.'

Paling, Dixie breathed in deep. 'It was an awful mistake. We were both upset. You'd been drinking. I was concerned, trying to comfort you…things just got out of hand. What more is there to say?'

'Are you telling me that you went to bed with me because you felt *sorry* for me?' César prompted with wrathful incredulity.

Dixie moved her head in a helpless gesture of confusion. 'I don't know... Apart from the obvious, I don't *know* why I did it!' she finally confessed.

'"Apart from the obvious"? What does that cover?' César demanded suspiciously.

'The lust bit,' Dixie whispered, marvelling that he hadn't grasped that for himself. 'I just get really carried away when you kiss me.'

The thunderous silence pulsed.

César settled his lean hands to her shoulders, raised her upright and turned her round. His stunning eyes locked into her mortified gaze like guided missiles. He bent his arrogant dark head and kissed her. Stars exploded in the darkness behind her lowered eyelids. Fireworks blazed up in a shower of sparks inside her. Her legs went hollow; her mind went blank.

César held her back from him, retaining a steadying hold on her slight shoulders. Deceptively indolent dark eyes surveyed her bemused expression. 'It's the sort of problem we need to work on together, Dixie.'

'I thought you'd be furious with me for taking advantage of you when you weren't quite sober,' she admitted in bewilderment.

César tautened, lashes dropping very low over glinting eyes. 'I'm not remotely sexist, and I'm remarkably resilient.'

Still struggling to understand why he had kissed her, Dixie tensed when he reached for her hand. He slid the diamond engagement ring on to her finger. 'You left it in my bathroom. Jasper will be expecting to see it.'

And only then did she realise why he had kissed her and why he wasn't furious. They still had to pretend to be engaged for Jasper's benefit. So when César closed a seemingly possessive hand over hers on the way downstairs she wasn't surprised. It was all part of the act.

'I didn't like to mention it before,' she confided. 'But I overheard you and Jasper talking—'

César glanced at her enquiringly. 'How much did you hear?'

Dixie looked awkward. 'Enough to know that it was going badly. You let Jasper back you into a corner—'

'I did...did I?'

'Well, you know you did,' Dixie pointed out ruefully. 'Telling Jasper that you'd marry me next week could've got us into a very difficult situation!'

Dark colour sprang up over César's spectacular cheekbones. He opened his mouth as if he was about to say something really cutting, and she stiffened. Then something strange happened. He looked at her. He sealed his lips again, veiled his eyes and simply shrugged a shoulder, expressively conceding the point.

'We'll have to tell him the truth when he's recovering from his op,' Dixie sighed. 'I think he'll understand why we did it.'

César's lean fingers gripped hers rather more tightly. 'Slight change of subject here, before we join Jasper,' he murmured smoothly. 'When we made love—'

Dixie bristled like a cornered animal, suddenly finding the hunter on her trail again. 'I thought we weren't going to discuss that again!'

'Just this once...' César studied her with broodingly intent and incisive dark eyes. 'I had this weird and wonderful idea that it might be something *more* than lust.'

Dixie reddened, humiliated by what she read into that admission but determined to assure him that she was not so foolish. 'You really don't need to worry about that, César.'

'I...don't?'

Dixie stared miserably down at their linked hands, thinking what a joke they were. 'I'm not silly enough to think that being physically attracted to someone is the same as being in love. Scott's still the only guy for me,' she swore vehemently.

César dropped her hand and bit out a sardonic laugh. 'You were with *me*, not him!' he derided.

'I'm pretty ashamed of that,' Dixie mumbled chokily.

'So you should be,' César confirmed in a suddenly savage undertone. 'Let me tell you, if you were in love with me I'd have an armed guard on you at all times. I wouldn't trust a woman as dippy and disloyal as you out of my sight!'

'But I don't even have a relationship with Scott yet,' she protested in her own defence.

'And if *I* have anything to do with it you never will!' César shot back at her chillingly.

Bemused by that assurance, Dixie finally worked up the courage to look up. César looked outraged. She was nailed to the spot by silvered eyes as piercing and threatening as knives.

'You used me,' César condemned fiercely. 'I don't let anybody do that.'

'How did I use you?' she gasped strickenly, seriously out of her depth and fighting to comprehend how she had angered him to such an extent.

'*Santo cielo*…like a bloody dry run for Scott! And to think I was worried about the fact that I hadn't taken any precautions!' César sent her a glittering look of what could only be described as pure loathing.

'Precautions?' Dixie was still working through the astonishing concept of César being some sort of sexual experiment, and not doing very well.

'Of course you're already on the pill, prepared for Scott,' César assumed with even greater scorn. 'The last thing you were going to risk was an accidental pregnancy, and I'm grateful…don't think I'm not! But when this fiasco is over I want you out of my life like you were never there in the first place!'

Dumbfounded by the number of contradic- tions, unexpected attacks and freewheeling as- sumptions coming her way, and hopelessly con- fused, Dixie watched César stride off, aggression radiating from every taut line of his lithe, pow- erful frame. She followed at a slower pace. She *wasn't* taking the contraceptive pill. The risk of a pregnancy hadn't even occurred to her. Confronted with that daunting reality, she went into even deeper shock.

Without warning, César wheeled round and strode back to her. Closing his hand back over hers again, he released his breath in a fractured hiss. Grim dark eyes gazed down into hers. 'I'm sorry…I had no right to attack you like that.'

Shaken by the gruff apology, Dixie muttered in a stifled voice. 'It's OK. I understand.'

'I don't think you do,' César said flatly.

But she did, she thought wretchedly. Over the past twelve hours everything had gone haywire. Sudden intimacy had brought down the barriers between them, and now the barriers had to be raised again. But no wonder César had been so on edge when he was worrying about whether or not he might have got her pregnant. Right then she decided to let him continue believing that he didn't need to worry about that possibility. She told herself that it was unlikely that one rash act would lead to the conception of a child, and stamped down hard on her anxiety. This morning she had to smile like a woman in love and newly engaged. Not one hint of the divisions between them could be revealed in Jasper's presence.

Jasper was waiting for them in a sunlit courtyard beneath the shade of a giant casuarina tree. With a wide smile on his creased face, he rose to his feet. 'Now don't tell me that I should've stayed in bed. Father Navarro is joining us for lunch.'

In the act of settling Dixie into a chair behind the beautifully set table, César stilled. 'Father Navarro?'

'So that we can set a date for the wedding. I gave him a call this morning. We haven't got time to waste. Eduardo wants me into that clinic within the next two weeks!' Patently unaware of the bombshell he had dropped on them both, Jasper sank back down into his seat, exuding an air of happy complacency.

CHAPTER EIGHT

As JASPER cheerfully suggested that César pour the wine, Dixie struggled not to visually betray what a shock she had just received.

'Don't look so disapproving, César,' Jasper scolded gently. 'One glass of wine won't do me any harm. This is a very special occasion.'

'Jasper…I seriously doubt that you need the excitement of a wedding night now.' César filled the crystal glasses with an admirably steady hand.

'Nonsense. I don't want you both feeling that you have to put things off until *after* my op! I'm fit enough for a quiet family affair.' A slight frown of strain formed on Jasper's worn features as he studied them both. 'Oh dear, have I taken too much of a liberty in contacting Father Navarro?'

César gave him an amused smile that impressed Dixie to death. 'Of course you haven't.' He glanced fleetingly at Dixie. 'Jasper and the village priest are old cronies, *cara*. He was sure to share our news with him first.'

Jasper relaxed again. 'You'll throw a big reception for all your friends once you're back in London, but a private ceremony here is much more your style, César. You won't be bothered by any paparazzi in this neck of the woods.'

Dixie suddenly grasped two things. Jasper was throwing himself into this wedding idea to take his mind off his coming surgery. He was also very much afraid that he wasn't going to survive the operation.

'You'll be fine. Apart from this little heart thing, you're in great condition for a man of your age,' she told him, as if he had spoken his fear out loud.

'Dixie reads me like a book,' Jasper told César rather smugly.

'You think a lot alike,' César remarked, without any expression at all.

And then the village priest arrived. For the two older men it was a jovial meal. Dixie kept on finding her mind drifting off the dialogue. She watched César, in awe at his self-control, his ease of speech, his ability to hide his horror at the situation in which they now found themselves. She kept on waiting for him to casually produce some clever reason which would regrettably make such a wedding out of the question in the near future, but César made not the slightest attempt.

Indeed, throughout that meal she could not drag her attention from César. That lean, strong face, the shard of sunlight that gleamed over his blue-black hair every time he threw his well-shaped head back, the warmth in the beautiful dark eyes she had once thought so cold when he looked at his godfather. He was putting on the show of the century for Jasper's sake.

By the time Father Navarro took his leave, a date only five days away had been settled on for the ceremony. Jasper went indoors for a nap. As his quiet footsteps receded, Dixie suddenly rose from the table and walked away, dragging in great gasps of the hot, still air as her tension slowly drained away, only to leave her in a state of disbelief.

Standing by the wall bounding the courtyard, she looked beyond the gorgeous terraced gardens spread out below to the magnificent view of the lushly wooded mountains. And she thought, Now César is about to tell me that we have no choice but to get married.

César paused several feet away, studying her with veiled dark eyes. 'You're furious with me.'

Dixie turned a strained profile to him, shaken reproach in her troubled blue eyes. 'You got us into this. Somehow I assumed you'd magically get us out of it again.'

'If I'd argued Jasper would've suspected I was having second thoughts about marrying you, and then he would've been upset. I couldn't risk it.'

'I care very much about Jasper, but I don't want to go to the lengths of a church wedding to placate him!' Dixie admitted starkly.

'We can get an annulment later.' César moved soundlessly closer, his brilliant eyes silver-bright slivers beneath his lush ebony lashes. 'I know you didn't bargain on this, and I'm not about to try and browbeat you into it. I realise that I'm asking you for a really huge favour.'

Her attention locked to his strikingly serious features, the stark tension etched into his fabulous bone structure, and something inside her just began to melt like butter left out under the sun.

'César, I—'

'*Please*…I need you to do this for me,' César breathed with roughened sincerity.

Dixie collided with his eyes, and a wave of such physical craving consumed her that it was a literal agony not to be in his arms. Shocked by that awareness, she trembled and twisted her head away. 'OK…it'll just be for a few weeks. Then we'll be back in London and we can just tell Jasper that it didn't work out.'

'I swear you won't regret this decision.'

Involuntarily, Dixie stole a glance at him. A slashing charismatic smile had driven the tension from his startlingly handsome features. As a burst of heat ignited in the pit of her stomach she lowered her gaze again, appalled by the power he had to disturb her. A power he wasn't even trying to exercise, a natural power he had simply been born with.

'There's just one thing you could do to make things a little easier,' she heard herself say stiffly.

'Name it.'

'Could we try and avoid each other as much as possible?'

For a split second César looked stunned.

Conscious that she had been clumsy, Dixie dropped her head and added, 'I just think it would make us both more comfortable.'

'You didn't seem particularly uncomfortable over lunch,' César remarked very softly. 'In fact you never took your eyes off me once.'

There he was again, seeking reassurance that she wasn't getting keen on him, Dixie reflected in mortification, her cheeks flaming. 'I was acting.'

'I should've thought of that. So you were imagining I was Scott?' he prompted in a roughened undertone.

Too embarrassed to look at him, Dixie interpreted that fracturing intonation as one of immense amusement. 'What else?'

*   *   *

Dixie's reflection in the tall cheval mirror took her breath away. Three days earlier César had had a selection of wedding dresses flown in, complete with a seamstress to make any necessary alterations on the spot. Just another prop for Jasper's benefit, Dixie had gathered. But seeing herself in full bridal regalia now, on her wedding day, was somehow something else entirely...

Jasper had insisted on loaning her a diamond tiara that had belonged to his mother. The jewels glittered like a wreath of stars in her upswept hair. And the gown? The gown was a perfect dream. Ivory silk enhanced by delicate embroidery skimmed her breasts, hugged her tiny waist and fell softly down to feet sheathed in gold embroidered shoes straight out of *Cinderella*.

Over the past five days Dixie had scarcely seen César, except in Jasper's presence. On César's side, keeping up an act had demanded little more than an impressive air of concerned interest in her wellbeing, and circumspect walks in the grounds after dinner.

'Jasper doesn't trust us to be alone,' César had gritted with a flash of outrage while his godfather strolled about in the courtyard above them like an eagle-eyed chaperone. 'What does he think I'm about to do? Drag you under the trees like a randy teenager?'

Recalling that incredulous outburst the previous evening, Dixie could not help smiling as she was ushered out of her room by Ermina, who had insisted on helping her to dress. Dear Jasper, she thought fondly. He didn't trust César an inch on the moral restraint front. Her smile slowly ebbed. Jasper really had nothing to worry about. That fateful night of passion would never be repeated.

Jasper watched Dixie come down the stairs with immense pride. 'You look superb, my dear.'

He handed her out into the waiting car as if she was a queen, and the run down the steep mountain road to the tiny church on the outskirts of the village slumbering in the heat of midday took only minutes. Jolted by the appearance of a photographer, to record her entrance on Jasper's arm, Dixie was a bundle of nerves when she mounted the shallow steps clutching her beautiful bouquet.

As the ceremony began, César finally turned to look at her. His dark, deep-set eyes flared silver, and he didn't turn away again. Eduardo Arribas, standing up as best man, had to give him a suggestive nudge when it was time to put the ring on her finger. Dixie was conscious of nothing but the quiet words of the service and César, devastatingly tall and sensationally attractive in an elegant charcoal-grey pinstripe suit.

She was leaving the church before she remembered to remind herself that it was all just a masquerade and not real at all. The photographer made them pose, and when they finally climbed into the car that would waft them back to the house for the wedding breakfast, she expected César to say something very cynical along the lines of, I'm glad that charade's over!

'You look absolutely incredible in that dress,' César breathed huskily instead.

'You don't have to pretend when we're on our own.'

'I'm not pretending—'

'Yes, you are. You know you are…like when you told me I had really stunning eyes,' she reminded him ruefully. 'You can switch off the act until we have to get out of the car again.'

In receipt of that dauntingly prosaic assurance, César murmured almost aggressively, 'You *do* have gorgeous eyes.'

Dixie sighed. 'Why are you carrying on like this?'

César met her frankly reproachful gaze with shimmering dark eyes that blazed a heat trail of intense sexual awareness through her. Dixie quivered. The atmosphere was suddenly so raw with leaping tension she couldn't breathe. Her mind filled with wanton imagery of their brief intimacy only days earlier. The hot, drugging glory of being in his arms. The wondrous, incredible sensation of that lean, powerful body moving over hers. In the grip of such memories, Dixie shifted on the seat, stabbed by guilty excitement.

And when César curved a lean-fingered hand to her waist and drew her close memory and reality converged, and there was not a thought in her head that she shouldn't do what she so desperately wanted to do. He crushed her soft mouth under his with devouring hunger. With scant ceremony, Dixie speared her hands possessively into his thick black hair and pulled him to her. Her thundering heartbeat merged with his and slowly, very slowly, they disappeared below the level of the car windows until they were lying full-length on the back seat.

Some timeless period later, after a bout of fevered kissing that left them both struggling for oxygen, César raised his head. 'The car's parked,' he remarked with a slight frown. 'The driver's gone.'

As César raised himself, taking her with him, Dixie surfaced, almost senseless from the depths of an all-encompassing passion and with her tiara askew. With deft hands César eased the tiara free, straightened her tumbled hair and slotted the tiara back into place.

'I think we'd better make our entrance…you can't have a wedding breakfast without the bride and groom, *cara mia*.' A heartbreaker of a smile curved César's wide, sensual mouth. As her heart gave a violent lurch, that smile set Dixie back at least five minutes in the recovery process.

César handed her out and smoothed down the folds of her gown as if they had all the time in the world. Then, before she could even catch her breath, he bent down and swept her up into his arms. 'What—?'

'Tradition, *cara*. Relax,' he teased, reading her anxious face with instant understanding and amusement. 'If you ever went on a diet, I'd forcefeed you with chocolate fudge cake every night.'

Dixie had never heard that teasing intonation from César before. It poleaxed her. And she was even more taken aback by the revelation that César could do something as distinctly uncool as kiss her breathless in the back of a car while their few guests waited for them to emerge.

In a decided daze, she let him carry her into the house, for all the world like a real bride on her wedding day. Hovering in the imposing shaded entrance, Jasper watched them approach with unconcealed contentment.

As they drew level he smiled, and said in a cheerful undertone, 'Bruce flew in with your mail, César. He also brought an unexpected visitor, whom I'm sure will be very much appreciated. I haven't shared your news yet. I love to surprise people!'

And indeed, as César strode into the comparative dimness of the hall, Dixie's beautiful ivory gown trailing across him like a banner, Jasper certainly succeeded in his wish to see people surprised.

César's executive assistant, Bruce Gregory, moved forward first, focused on Dixie in her wedding dress and fell still with a dropped jaw.

'Close your mouth, Bruce,' César murmured gently to the younger man. 'You look like one of Dixie's fish.'

The unexpected visitor pushed past Bruce. A very glamorous blonde wearing an eye-catching leopard print skirt and matching crop top that exposed her exotically jewelled navel. She let her breath escape in a startled hiss when she saw the bride and groom. Momentarily, her beautiful face was a study of complete disbelief.

'Petra?' Dixie exclaimed in delighted amazement. 'César, this is my sister, Petra!'

Brilliant dark eyes narrowing, César came to a halt and surveyed the now brightly smiling blonde. 'Hello, Petra,' he drawled smoothly. 'What a shame you had to miss the ceremony by such a narrow margin!'

'Petra…this is César…César Valverde,' Dixie announced, with considerable pride in her ability to introduce her famous sister to someone she felt to be worthy of her notice.

'Everybody knows who César Valverde is,' Petra Sinclair remarked with a patronising look of amusement she attempted to share with César, but César simply stared steadily back at her, not a muscle moving on his darkly handsome face.

'How did you find out where I was?' Dixie demanded, still in César's arms and momentarily blinded when the photographer stepped forward to take a flash photo of their entrance.

'You left a forwarding address, darling. And when I showed up at César's house and ran into Brucie, I persuaded him to let me hitch a ride out here with him.'

'Brucie' angled a somewhat weak and apologetic smile in his employer's direction. César sent him a flashing glance that made him tense. 'Congratulations, César,' he managed, nonetheless. 'And Dixie, my very warmest good wishes. I have to confess…I didn't see this development on the horizon.'

'You said it first,' Petra said, rather shrilly. 'But don't you just love weddings? I know *I* do!'

César slowly lowered Dixie to the floor. 'Excuse me, *cara*,' he murmured in a quiet aside. 'I have an urgent call to make.'

Petra crossed the hall and closed an arm round her much smaller stepsister. 'I really have missed having you around,' she confided, while Jasper looked on with warm approval of such sisterly affection.

Surprised by Petra's unusual demonstrativeness, Dixie glowed. 'I've missed you too. How was California?'

As Jasper moved away, Petra dropped her smile and gave a petulant shrug. 'It didn't work out, and then I landed back in London, expecting you to be able to put me up—'

'Oh, *no!*' Dixie was dismayed.

'And then when I realised you were in Spain, with dear old Jasper, I just crossed my fingers and *prayed* there'd be room for an extra house guest!' Petra studied Dixie's concerned and guilty face with cool green eyes. 'As I'm really broke right now, I had no choice.'

'No, *of course*, you didn't,' Dixie agreed fervently, hoping that César and Jasper wouldn't mind Petra staying on while she herself looked forward to an opportunity to catch up with all her sister's news.

César returned to her side, and Dixie noticed that Bruce was now welded to a phone on the far side of the hall.

Although Dixie would have appreciated a few minutes to talk to her sister in private, she could see it wasn't possible when everybody was waiting for their meal. At the table, she had Jasper on one side of her and César on the other. Petra ended up beside Father Navarro, who seemed to be rather heavily into talking about the joys of early matrimony and large families. Unfortunately Petra made several rather inappropriate comments, and then sank into a silence punctuated only by large yawns.

'I'm just so pleased Petra is here,' Dixie shared shyly with César as he put his hand over hers to cut the beautiful wedding cake. 'Obviously she's really tired, and she's not too comfortable with men of the cloth, but isn't she just gorgeous?'

'So that's the shade of blonde hair you hanker after? It wouldn't suit you at all,' César informed her in a charged undertone. 'You're not hankering after the butterfly tattoo and the body piercing as well, are you?'

'Well, I must say—'

'All that stuff hurts like hell. You'd be in real agony,' César interrupted, watching Dixie pale. 'Your stepsister must be very brave.'

'Yes, she is. Things didn't work out for her in California, but she's just taking it on the chin.' Dixie sighed, full of sympathy.

After the meal, Dixie went to the cloakroom to tidy her hair. When she emerged, Petra was pacing the floor outside, an angry look on her face.

'I nearly fell asleep over that meal…I thought the punishment was never going to end!'

Curving a determined hand over her arm, Petra herded Dixie into the nearest empty room. Closing the door, her blonde stepsister rested back against it, widening her cat-green eyes meaningfully. '*You* and César Valverde married?' she questioned with a rather high-pitched laugh. 'I am gobsmacked—and obviously it changes my plans. I can hardly stay here when you've just got hitched!'

Dixie stared at her in surprise. 'Why ever not?'

'Use your brain, Dixie,' Petra said thinly. 'This is Jasper's house, and now you'll be taking off on some extravagant honeymoon trip. I can scarcely plonk myself down here and wait for your return. I wouldn't want to anyway. I've never met so many pontificating old bores in one spot in my entire life!'

'This is actually César's house, Petra. It belonged to his late father, but Jasper has lived here for years.' Disconcerted as she was by such scorn, Dixie couldn't help being relieved that Petra wasn't instantly subjecting her to a barrage of awkward questions as to how she and César had contrived to get together. She really didn't want to lie to her sister. 'And since Jasper hasn't been too well, César and I won't be taking off anywhere.'

'Rather you than me. I can't stick nurse-maiding old folk, but I can see that this time it's paid off *very* well for you!' Sullen resentment flashed in Petra's eyes. 'Look, why don't you do me a favor and just give me a loan so that I can hightail it back out of this rural place and leave you to enjoy the fruits of your stupendously *good* marriage?'

In receipt of that pointedly derisive speech, Dixie frowned in growing bewilderment, wondering what had got into Petra, who was usually the life and soul of every social gathering. 'A…*loan*?'

'You just married an entire bank,' Petra spelt out with a curled lip.

Uneasy colour lit Dixie's cheeks. 'Petra, I couldn't possibly ask César to give you money—'

'Why not? Is the catch of the century tight with his mega-millions?'

'César settled the bills that you overlooked when you flew out to California,' Dixie countered uncomfortably, disturbed that her stepsister had yet to make any reference to the debts she had left behind her.

Petra stiffened. 'So César knows about all that?'

'Yes.'

Petra reddened angrily. 'It wasn't my fault that I got in such a mess!'

'No, I know it wasn't.' But Petra seemed to have a very cavalier attitude to other people's money, and that did trouble Dixie.

Soothed by Dixie's agreement, Petra sniffed. 'Well, if you'll excuse me for saying so, I've got no desire to hang around here playing gooseberry to my kid sister!'

'If you stayed, it wouldn't be like that... I mean...' Dixie floundered '...our marriage isn't like that.'

But as soon as she said that she recalled the heated embrace she and César had shared in the car. She flushed. Had César been acting for Jasper's benefit again? Or was César just not very good at maintaining a platonic relationship? Or was it even remotely possible that César could still be as tempted by her as she was by him? She discounted that third possibility and opted to believe the first. He had just been *acting* passionate.

'What is that supposed to mean?' Petra demanded very drily.

'César only married me to please Jasper. It's really just a pretend marriage to keep Jasper happy until he gets over his coming surgery,' Dixie heard herself confess tautly. 'So there would be no question of you needing to feel like a gooseberry.'

Petra gave her an arrested look, green eyes gleaming with sudden satisfaction. 'Now that does make more sense to me. After all, what the hell would a guy like César Valverde see in a little dowdy dumpling like you? No offence intended,' she added carelessly as Dixie paled, 'but let's face it, you're no oil painting, and he *is*—'

'Yes,' Dixie cut in tightly, really hurt by that 'dumpling' label.

'The guy is absolutely gorgeous,' Petra continued, carefully examining her own striking reflection in a nearby mirror. 'He's a hunk and he's loaded. Much more my type than yours.'

'I guess he is,' Dixie responded not quite evenly, studying the carpet, feeling very round and very small and horribly plain for the first time since César had worked what she had fondly imagined was a transformation of no mean order. You thought a new hairstyle and some fancy clothes could pull off a miracle? a little voice sounding remarkably like Petra's sneered. Are you for real?

'And César has got to be bored witless stuck here with you and that bunch of old fogies! And you really don't count, do you?' Petra said reflectively, as if her thoughts were far away. 'You're quite right. In the circumstances, there's no reason why I shouldn't stay. It might be fun to spend some time with you.'

Dixie focused on her stepsister's exotically embellished navel, shocked and concerned to discover that from the instant Petra had pointed out that she herself was much more César's type she hadn't really wanted her to stay any more. She was appalled by such a mean-minded prompting.

'And…have I got a surprise for you!' Petra continued, digging a hand into her fashionably tiny bag to produce a crumpled envelope.

At that point the door opened, framing César. Tall and dark and smiling. Even so Dixie sensed an oddly charged quality to his stance. His attention immediately went to her troubled face.

'Your ex-landlady passed it on to me.' Petra handed the letter to Dixie and sidestepped César with a vibrant smile to walk out of the room.

'What's that?' César demanded, striding forward.

Dixie's attention fell on the handwriting. 'Oh, my goodness, it's a letter from Scott!'

Eyes glittering like ice shards, César reached out a hand and snatched it from her again.

Dixie gave him an aghast look of complete bewilderment.

'*Dio*…' César scanned the postmark. 'He posted this from the airport!'

Bruce's voice intervened quietly from the doorway. 'Everything's organised, César.'

One of the maids chose that same moment to enter with a tray of coffee.

'Can I h-have my letter back, please?' Dixie stammered.

'Be my guest.' César returned the letter with precise cool and strolled across the room to join Bruce. 'Would you like some coffee? Help yourself. I need somebody really grounded around me at this minute, because whether you realise it or not, the most major event of my bride's day is now taking place. And this thrilling, unexpected joy, so thoughtfully provided by my stepsister-in-law? A letter from Scott.'

'He's never written to me before, César!' Not really listening, believing that he was teasing her again, and Bruce's presence quite passing her by, Dixie was busy tearing open the envelope. 'Oh, *no*!'

'He's dead?'

'Don't be silly, César. Scott wanted me to go round to his flat so that the repair man could fix his washing machine.'

'New York wasn't far enough,' César mused reflectively.

'But he's actually given me his phone number over there!' Dixie shared in genuine surprise. 'Imagine that!'

'The computer's using every line in the house at the minute,' César delivered flatly. 'And it costs a *fortune* to ring New York.'

'You're right. And then there's the time difference,' Dixie muttered vaguely, automatically glancing at César, as if she expected him to clarify that seeming technicality for her.

'Time differences confuse the hell out of me. You'd have to look it up...haven't a clue where. Get the hell out of here, Bruce,' César raked softly to his convulsed executive assistant, who, having emerged from sheer incredulity, was now struggling desperately hard not to laugh.

'I'd really have liked to know how Scott was getting on with his new job,' Dixie sighed, re-reading her three-line letter rather forlornly.

'He'll be having a whale of a time. New York is a very exciting place,' César murmured, evidently in an attempt to be comforting. 'It's full of sophisticated, gorgeous, unattached women.'

'Knowing Scott as I do,' Dixie mused absently, 'he's sure to be making the most of the experience.'

She was lost in her own thoughts. She no longer believed that she was in love with Scott, and was rather embarrassed by that reality now. How could she have known herself so little and contrived to assume so much?

Over the past week or so she had learnt a lot about herself, and grown up a fair bit too. While she'd been nursing her stepmother she simply hadn't had a social life. And when she'd arrived in London men hadn't exactly beaten a path to her door. So she'd developed a crush on Scott, a harmless but rather juvenile infatuation that had given her more pleasure than pain. After all, she'd enjoyed daydreaming about Scott and discussing him endlessly with anybody willing to listen. Not having a boyfriend hadn't seemed to matter while she had Scott to focus on, and goodness knows she had had nothing much else in her life, she conceded ruefully...

In the stretching silence, César watched Dixie like a hawk. Looking pale and unbearably sad as she inwardly acknowledged the end of an era, Dixie crushed the letter slowly between her fingers. For a normally sunny personality, the gesture seemed redolent of real drama.

'OK...you can phone Scott tonight.'

Emerging from her reverie in some surprise, Dixie encountered the full onslaught of César's penetrating dark eyes and struggled not to shiver in reaction. She wondered why he looked so tense, so...*guilty*? She immediately discarded that fleeting impression. What, after all, could César have to feel guilty about, today of all days? Jasper was happy as a sandboy.

'Thanks…I'd like to wish him well,' she admitted.

'I'm afraid we'll have to leave soon. And, beautiful as that dress is, I imagine you'll want to change,' César continued with supreme cool.

That statement certainly grabbed Dixie's attention. 'Leave?' she queried. 'Leave to go where?'

'We'll be spending the next few days at another location.'

'Like…like on a honeymoon?' Dixie prompted in undisguised horror, quick to catch his drift in spite of his avoidance of that emotive label. 'But I assumed that with Jasper unwell—'

'Eduardo Arribas will be staying while we're away. Jasper naturally expects us to *want* to spend time alone together.'

Colliding with César's stunning dark eyes, Dixie reddened and looked away. 'But it's going to be so awkward…being alone, I mean.'

'Pack plenty of books,' César advised bracingly.

While Dixie was getting changed, Petra came upstairs to find her again.

A bright smile suggesting a considerable improvement in her mood, her stepsister breezed into her room and broke straight into speech. 'Since you *are* going away, César's offered me the use of a condo in an exclusive development on the coast! I've decided to take him up on it. He knows it's too quiet here for me.'

Dixie smiled as she slid her feet into shoes. 'That was really kind of him.'

'Kind? Oh, I don't think it was just that—and I'm so relieved you told me the truth about this marriage of yours *because*...' As Petra fulminatingly scrutinised Dixie, in her scarlet designer sundress with its flirty hem, her green eyes sparkled with more than a hint of malice. 'I think César fancies me like mad!'

Dixie's stomach turned over sickly. The colour drained from her face and she turned away to hide her reaction.

'I can always tell when a man wants me,' Petra continued with conviction. 'When César first saw me downstairs he just froze; he didn't show any reaction at all. Of course he *couldn't*, could he? Not when it was supposed to be his wedding day! And he's clever, isn't he? Good at concealing things...'

'Yes, he is,' Dixie acknowledged gruffly, her throat closing over. And suddenly, with a sinking heart, she knew exactly why she was hurting—but not why she was so shocked by Petra's announcement. After all, most men were attracted to Petra. Her stepsister wasn't just glamorous and sexy; she was a fun person to be with. So why had she got the idea that César was less than impressed by Petra? Had that been wishful thinking?

'In fact, I think César's already regretting getting himself into this crazy charade with you just to keep the old boy content!' Petra opined drily. 'Still, like you said, that'll be over soon, and César will be free to do as he likes...and I'll certainly be free to do it with him!'

CHAPTER NINE

DIXIE never once asked César where they were to spend their brief honeymoon. In a melodramatic mood, new to her experience, her sole concern was getting César away from Petra as fast as possible. She could not have borne the strain of seeing them together, watching her stepsister flirt, watching César cloak his eyes, shutter that lean, dark, fallen-angel face to conceal his desire to respond in kind...

She had never dreamt she could feel so sick with jealousy or be torn by so many deeply unpleasant emotions. Nothing could have prepared her for the shameful knowledge that for a split second she had actually felt she hated Petra, and had wished her stepsister would vanish in a puff of smoke like the wicked fairy!

But within an hour of their departure Dixie's anger was directed solely at herself. She had fallen head over heels in love with César, but she had cravenly refused to confront that reality. Stubborn denial hadn't protected her, it had just left her out of touch with her own emotions and defenceless. The pain she had tried to evade she was feeling now. César was never going to love her back.

Her love had been an accident waiting to happen. His sheer animal sex appeal had overwhelmed her, and then she had started thinking about him and worrying about him and caring about him. All common sense had deserted her and she had ended up in bed with him, foolishly risking pregnancy and even greater heartbreak.

If she had never experienced that incredible intimate closeness with César she would have been less vulnerable. Whereas *now*... Dixie reflected with intense shame, she couldn't even look at that lean, powerful body of his, exquisitely packaged by superb tailoring, without feeling quite sick with longing and desire.

The helicopter delivered them to the airport, where they boarded the jet. Dixie pretended to doze during the flight. Put aboard a second helicopter in Athens, she was merely grateful that conversation was impossible, but was surprised that César had chosen to travel so far afield when a more convenient location would surely have satisfied Jasper's expectations.

When they had made a final landing, César lifted Dixie out of the helicopter. They were only yards away from a golden stretch of sand and surging sparkling blue sea. The pilot loaded their luggage into the beach buggy parked above the quay.

'It's a private island,' César divulged with considerable satisfaction. 'And we have it all to ourselves.'

Of course, Dixie thought without surprise. He wouldn't want other people around. He wouldn't want to have to pretend they were normal honeymooners, all over each other like a rash and deliriously happy. Parting her lips, she said as much before she could think better of it.

'You've got a point,' César agreed, studying her strained profile and the down-curve of her lips. 'Delirious happiness is not a realistic goal at this point in time.'

As Dixie climbed into the beach buggy she flushed guiltily. 'I've been a real drag all the way here, haven't I?'

'No,' César countered steadily. 'You've just been quiet.'

Dixie frowned, trying to recall when she had last really spoken to César. They had been leaving the house. 'You would've found Petra much better company,' she heard herself say tightly now. 'Maybe you should've dropped me at the condo on the coast and brought her here instead. Jasper wouldn't have known any different!'

That outburst took César as much by surprise as it did Dixie. Clamping her hand to her mouth, she stared at him in horror over the top of her fingers. 'Just joking!' she added abruptly.

His brilliant dark gaze narrowed and gleamed as if he had suddenly struck gold. 'Where did you get the idea that I was interested in your stepsister?'

Dixie stiffened, lashes concealing her stricken gaze. 'Most men are.'

'I'm not most men.'

But he *was*. Long tall blondes with a lot of temperament were his trademark. And for the few minutes it had taken them to say their good-byes and depart Dixie had carefully observed César's behaviour. He had more or less ignored Petra. Men did not simply ignore Petra when she was smiling and being genuinely amusing. Such a complete lack of reaction had convinced Dixie that César was indeed very much attracted to her stepsister but determined to hide the fact.

In the shimmering silence that rewarded his assurance that he was *not* one of the common herd, César's wide, sensual mouth suddenly clenched hard. Breathing in deep, he sent the buggy up the hill at a roaring pace and drew it to a grinding halt outside an amazing house that was, until the very last bend, all but concealed by a magnificent belt of specimen trees and wild lush planting.

'Oh, this is really lovely,' Dixie whispered shakily, knowing that men didn't relish comments on their driving skills.

His bronzed profile taut, shimmering eyes veilcd, César sprang out, hauled out all their luggage in one go and strode to the door with it, ferocious tension splintering from every movement.

All too well aware that she should have kept quiet about her suspicions, Dixie followed him at a slower pace into the cool tiled hall. What has possessed her? she asked herself miserably. Naturally César would not wish to confess that he was attracted to Petra when he had already more or less accidentally shared a bed with Dixie and there wasn't the slightest chance of him getting together with her stepsister in the near future.

'I had hoped to avoid admitting it,' César breathed in a driven undertone. 'But I disliked Petra on sight. It was instantaneous.'

Falling still, Dixie gazed at him in astonishment.

'In fact there is a five-letter word that sums up my exact opinion of your stepsister, who wasn't under my roof an hour before she began causing trouble!' César slung in raw-edged addition.

'A f-five-letter word...?' Dixie stammered.

'But out of respect for your affection for her I would prefer not to use it.'

He couldn't mean... But, absorbing the icy glitter of his eyes, Dixie registered that he did mean exactly that, and she reeled in shock. But out of the shock emerged the most giddy sense of relief she had ever experienced.

'Right now,' César murmured with sudden surprising intensity, 'I don't have another woman in my life, and—'

At that precise moment, his mobile phone buzzed.

With an expressive sound of impatience César answered it, and immediately tensed. Dixie was close enough to recognise the pitch of a woman's voice. Dark colour accentuated César's slashing cheekbones. He glanced around himself like a male in dire need of an escape hatch, and finally strode out through the front door again with something less than his usual cool. 'It's not very convenient for me to talk at this moment,' she heard him confide grittily.

He leant up against the side of the beach buggy, wide shoulders rigid, his entire attention fiercely pinned to Dixie, who was lugging her case noisily upstairs one step at a time.

'Here, let me take that,' César insisted when he caught up with her. 'That was Lisette on the phone. I...I told her I'd got married.'

'I suppose it's as good an excuse as any you'll ever have.' Dixie surveyed him with reproachful eyes. 'But couldn't you have come up with something kinder?'

'Kinder?' César repeated, very much as though he wasn't quite getting the response he had expected.

'What an awful shock for the poor woman! One minute you're having an affair with her, and the next—'

'The relationship hadn't progressed as far as the bedroom…and now it's over, OK?' César cut in, ruthlessly blunt in his exasperation.

Embarrassed, Dixie reddened and averted her eyes. 'I really don't think that's any of my business, César. I'm sorry, I shouldn't have said what I did,' she told him apologetically. 'It's so confusing, this pretending and then not having to pretend…after a while pretending begins to feel like the real thing, and before I know where I am, I'm being too personal again.'

'Maybe we should just keep on pretending. It might be more interesting…' César cast wide the single door off the landing.

Dixie was already puzzled by the absence of any other doors in so apparently spacious a villa. 'Interesting? My goodness!' she gasped after one astonished glimpse at the vast and luxurious bedroom stretching before her.

Maybe there was another bedroom downstairs. She turned round. César had already gone down to get the rest of the luggage. On the ground floor, Dixie discovered an incredibly opulent reception area, an elegant dining room and a superb kitchen with a fridge full of food. She finally accepted that there was only one bed in the entire house.

César rejoined her and helped himself to a rather large brandy. Dixie took a deep breath. 'César, when I was upstairs I just couldn't help...er...noticing that there's only one...'

While she had been speaking César had downed the brandy in one unappreciative gulp. He straightened his shoulders and angled a shuttered look at her. 'I think this would be a good time for you to ring Scott,' he said flatly.

'Oh...yes, right,' Dixie muttered, distracted by that suggestion.

Five minutes later she dialled the number, and was delighted when Scott answered immediately. Scott was surprised to hear from her, but really, really pleased.

'You're homesick? Oh, Scott, how awful!' Dixie sighed with loads of sympathy, while watching César ram back the sliding patio doors with what struck her as quite unnecessary force. 'Tell me about the New York office... But you're really smart too, Scott, don't let people intimidate you,' she urged supportively as César hovered several feet away with the most strange aura of controlled menace, his lean, strong face rigid, bright eyes mere slivers of silver. 'Of course you'll cope. I know you'll be absolutely brilliant. I have every faith in you. I always have had. You can do *anything* you want to do!'

César suddenly strode past her into the kitchen. The door slammed. Dixie flinched. She heard a dulled thud, a muffled oath and then an unholy silence stretched. She stared in real dismay at that closed door. Was César OK? Had he fallen and hurt himself? The door opened a crack again and she relaxed slightly.

'Yes, I'm still here, Scott,' Dixie continued a little weakly.

'You're such a special person, Dixie. I feel better already,' Scott told her gratefully. 'I'll take you out to dinner when I get home.'

'Dinner? Oh I'd love that,' Dixie assured him, rather eager to get off the phone now.

'Can you give me your number?'

'Well, I'm in Greece right now,' Dixie explained uncertainly.

'What are you doing there?' Scott sounded aghast. 'Are you on holiday?'

'A sort of working holiday.' As the kitchen door crashed shut again, Dixie concluded her call.

She sped into the kitchen. Ashen-faced and breathing rapidly, César was leaning back against the units, blood dripping from a cut on his left hand. 'Oh, your poor hand!' Dixie moaned in instant agony for his suffering.

Reaching straight for the first-aid kit prominently displayed, Dixie broke into it. 'Let me get that cleaned up—'

'Don't fuss…it's just a graze!' he grated.

Dixie hauled over a chair and dragged him down into it. He looked as if he was about to faint. It was his thumb, quite a deep slash. 'This might need stitches—'

'Nonsense…it's nothing.'

'How on earth did you do it?'

'I…*bumped* into something on the wall,' César advanced, with brooding grimness and eyes as unreadable as a black wall.

'Do you feel dizzy?'

'No,' he growled.

Dixie dealt with the cut with great efficiency.

'I suppose you were a girl guide.'

'Yes…' Dixie studied that lean brown hand, so dark against hers, and without the slightest warning was just overcome with strong emotion. He would have submitted to death by torture sooner than admit up-front that the sight of blood seriously challenged his ability to stay upright.

Without even thinking about it, she pressed her lips softly to the back of his hand.

César tensed, but when she tried to pull back he held on to her. 'I have a confession to make.'

Drowning in a wave of appalled mortification at the rather revealing liberty she had just taken, Dixie bowed her head.

'*I* had Scott sent to New York.'

'S-sorry?' Dixie stammered with a frown.

'The minute you told me about Scott I was worried that you might be tempted to put being with him ahead of Jasper,' César revealed harshly. 'So I called in a favour with a partner in his firm and arranged to have him sent abroad. All it took was a two-minute phone call.'

Genuinely horrified by that level of cold-blooded calculation, Dixie lifted her head and gazed into fathomless dark eyes.

'And I'd be lying if I said I was sorry,' César completed.

'I'm just…I'm just so shocked by this…' Registering that it didn't seem quite right to still be holding hands with César after such a revelation, Dixie tugged her fingers free with a tearing sense of loss and confusion she despised. 'You are, without doubt, the most dreadfully selfish person,' she told him unsteadily. 'I can only hope that this temporary transfer at least benefits

Scott's career, because so far he is not enjoying himself over there!'

'I think I'm beginning to feel sorry,' César remarked thoughtfully. 'Not sorry I did what I did, but sorry I succumbed to the disastrous desire to confess.'

'That doesn't surprise me in the slightest,' Dixie said unevenly. 'Don't you *ever* think of people as individuals?'

'I'm getting the image of an exceedingly *wet* individual where Scott's concerned,' César shared very drily. 'I hand him the opportunity of a lifetime and he gets homesick after a week in one of the most exciting cities in the world!'

'That's not the point,' Dixie protested. 'People are more than just puppets you can manipulate!'

'Isn't it strange that I always had this sentimental belief that a free confession won an instant pardon?' César drawled as he rose to his feet with controlled grace.

Dixie leapt up, her cheeks colouring at that response. There was a certain truth in that comeback. If César hadn't chosen to tell her what he had done, she would certainly never, ever have found out. She followed him back into the sitting room. 'Yes...well, actually I—'

'I think I'll go down to the beach for a while.' His darkly handsome features shuttered, César murmured drily. 'I need no mystic powers to divine that this is unlikely to be a wedding night to remember!'

Technically, it *was* their wedding night, Dixie recalled numbly. And she guessed that so far César hadn't found it very entertaining. On the trip here she had been a real wet blanket, and not much more fun since their arrival. In less than an hour she had preached at him twice. 'I'm sorry you're bored,' she whispered tightly, just as he reached the doors that led out to the grounds.

César stilled. 'I'm not bored.'

'Are you hungry?' Dixie pressed hopefully, guilty discomfiture and a very strong desire to keep him with her making her powerfully keen to feed him. 'I could make you something to eat.'

Against the backdrop of the magnificent sunset, César shook his arrogant dark head in apparent wonderment at the offer. 'I'm not hungry for food.'

Her brow indented. César turned back to her. Silhouetted against the strong light, broad shoulders sheathed in the finest pale linen, lean hips and long powerful thighs accentuated by expensive tailoring, he was achingly beautiful. Bronze skin, black hair, glittering dark eyes silvering as he tipped his proud head back. Her tummy twisted and her heart jumped, tension snaking through her as she succumbed to the compulsive need to stare.

'I'm hungry for you…' César murmured.

'For…for me?' Dixie's shaken voice was strained.

'Famished, ravenous, starving,' César extended, not quite levelly, dazzling eyes glinting over her like laser probes.

Her tummy flipped sky-high, her legs turning hollow.

'Just thought I'd mention it… You see, what was an awful mistake for you *wasn't* an awful mistake for me,' César spelt out very carefully.

Dixie couldn't take her eyes off him. She was paralysed to the spot. 'It…wasn't?'

'*I* thought the experience was sensational,' César confided huskily.

Dixie shivered as her full breasts stirred, their rosy peaks swelling into almost painful sensitivity. 'Possibly because you had been drinking—'

'No…and don't do that—don't sell yourself short!' César censured, bright eyes blazingly intent on her bemused face, his mouth twisting. 'A man can't fake his response to the woman he wants.'

And as she stared at him and divined his meaning, and involuntarily lowered her gaze, a soft little sound of sheer surprise escaped her parted lips. His arousal was boldly etched, and as she met his eyes again the devouring hunger there made liquid heat burn up between her slender thighs. In fact, so intense was that physical sensation she stumbled back a step in dismay.

'You couldn't trust me within a yard of that bed with you in it,' César admitted with unashamed candour. 'I would definitely pounce! I'll sleep down here.'

As he swung away, Dixie's face fell a mile. Yes, he really wanted her...well, sexually. The lust bit again. *Sensational?* A wanton tingle ran down her spine and her legs quivered. He was walking out of the door...why wasn't she stopping him? Sex for the sake of it—what he was used to, *all* he was used to, and the most he had ever required from a woman. But not enough for her. All wrong for her! She loved him too much already, was too vulnerable, too painfully aware that within weeks Jasper's recovery would lead to a complete separation.

But as César disappeared into the lengthening shadows he flung Dixie into emotional turmoil. She was so tempted to snatch at what he offered. What did she have to lose? She wanted him so much. More than pride, more than principle. And at that instant it was César's own ruthlessly cutting drawl which flooded her memory. 'You're so convinced you're going to fail, you won't even bother trying!'

Right, Dixie decided, her adrenalin fairly leaping to that challenge. Just for once she was going to take a risk and break all her own rules. She plucked the magnum of champagne from the ice bucket in the fridge, dug out a corkscrew and started down the hill to the beach, plotting every step of the way. He was scared of commitment, so she would have to set him free at the outset rather than give him the faintest hint that she was hoping for anything other than a casual affair. That way he would relax…

César was on the shore, staring out to sea. Kicking off her shoes, Dixie padded across the sand with a fast-beating heart, wishing he would hear her and turn round, but the soft rush of the surf concealed her approach. She trod right up to him and pressed the champagne bottle into his hand.

He spun with a startled frown.

Dixie planted the corkscrew into his other hand and addressed his chest. 'I thought it was sensational too…and I don't see any reason for you to sleep downstairs on a stupid squashy floral sofa—'

'Scott?' César almost whispered.

'He's in New York!' Dixie responded, quick as a flash. 'He's like—'

'Out of sight…out of mind?' César slotted in with rich cynicism.

'It's not like that, César—'

'*Dio mio*…why am I arguing?' César demanded in a raw undertone as he suddenly dropped both champagne and corkscrew and swept her up into his arms with devastating strength and enthusiasm.

'Absolutely no strings,' Dixie told him breathlessly, the warm, achingly familiar scent of him washing over her as she wrapped her arms round his neck and pushed her face against his shoulder. 'I'm not a committed sort of person,' she added, in case her first statement hadn't been enough to release him from any subconscious anxiety that she might be more clingy than his usual kind of lover.

César lifted her higher and crushed her soft mouth with fierce hunger under his. She went weak from head to toe. Urgently prying her lips apart, he kept on kissing her, but the whole tenor of the embrace changed. He went from passion to unexpected tenderness, running his mouth lightly over her swept down eyelids, her damp cheeks, before recapturing her reddened lips with a sweetness that was almost unbearable, his breath mingling with hers. And then, very slowly, he slid her down over his powerfully masculine frame until her bare feet hit the sand again.

As she looked up at him with unwittingly enquiring eyes, César framed her hectically flushed cheekbones with two big hands. 'Sand gets everywhere,' he murmured teasingly.

And he knew that. Of course he did. Nine years older than her, he was a lot more than nine years ahead of her in experience. But Dixie discovered that she didn't want to think about the other women César had had in his life, or of how very different she was from those other women. Not glossy, not glamorous, not sophisticated, not even blonde. She didn't fit the mould, and that scared her.

When they arrived in the bedroom she felt horrendously shy. She hadn't had to think about what she was doing the last time, hadn't had to take responsibility. But César reached for her with a knowing light in his beautiful dark eyes and drew her close. With deft hands he unzipped her dress, gently brushed the straps from her shoulders and let the garment fall to her feet.

His burnished gaze gleamed with rich appreciation over the strapless ivory silk bra and matching lace panties she wore. 'You're exquisite, *cara mia*,' he murmured very softly.

'You say all the right things…practice, I suppose,' Dixie conceded tautly.

A wolfish grin illuminated his mobile mouth, brilliant eyes glinting. 'You're so perfect for me. Nothing I do impresses you!'

'Oh, it does…' Dixie contradicted instantly, dark blue eyes anxious that he should think that, even as her susceptible heart lurched beneath the onslaught of that wonderful smile.

Catching her up in his arms, he laid her down on the magnificent canopied bed. Her breasts rising and falling with every shortened breath, she watched him peel off his clothes with fluid cool. Her heart pounded in her ears as the surging tide of longing dug deep, warming her cheeks, clenching her fingers in on her palms. His lithe, sun-darkened body had the balance and flow of a classic statue suddenly cloaked in living flesh and muscle, but no statue had ever been so rampantly male in his arousal.

'I just can't believe this is us,' she whispered, as a mental image flashed into her mind of César as he was at the bank. Ruthlessly cold, remote, reserved. The memory terrified her.

'Believe it,' César urged huskily, surveying her opulently feminine curves with reverent anticipation.

'But it's not really us…it's like time out of time…'

Lacing his fingers possessively into her tumbled hair, César tugged her into his arms. Suddenly she was trembling helplessly, shot through with need, shifting against his lean, hard length with leaping hunger. Moth to a candle-flame, she thought fearfully, and then, as he freed her breasts from their silk confinement and expertly caressed the tormentingly sensitive tips, she gasped, and the glory of simply feeling stopped all thought dead in its tracks.

'*Dio*…I love your body, *cara mia*,' César confessed with passionate intensity, and as he cupped her ripe curves he bent his dark head and let the tip of his tongue travel down between her proud breasts, licking the perspiration from her skin.

Her tummy contracted, excitement pulling at her. 'I never knew I could feel like this…' she gasped achingly.

His sure hands curved over her hips as he lifted her up to him and kissed her with unrestrained hunger and all-male dominance. Her every sense sang. He traced a slender trembling thigh to its apex, groaned with eloquent appreciation as he discovered the hot dampness even her panties couldn't conceal. He pressed his mouth hotly to the tiny pulse going crazy at her collarbone and gritted feverishly, 'Jasper was right to patrol the courtyard all those endless evenings…never had so many cold showers in my life!'

She kissed the top of his head, loving the silky density of his hair, the smell of him, the smoothness of his cheekbones below her palms, the interesting roughness beyond, and all the time the heat was pooling inside her, driving her increasingly crazy. 'Want you so much,' she moaned.

'How much?' César demanded with sizzling bite.

In the state she was in as he stripped away the silk and lace barrier still separating him from her she couldn't quantify such a thing. At that moment he was everything, the planet around which she spun like a satellite. 'Too much…'

'Not possible, *mi amore*.' He strung an enervating line of darting kisses over her squirmingly restive body, finding erotic places she hadn't known existed before, letting his fingertips smooth through the damp dark curls screening the hot core of her.

And then he relented and traced the silken flesh crying out for his touch, and her breath caught on a rising pant of sensual shock and she threw her head back, spine arching as the shameless pleasure took her in uncontrollable waves. She ached and she needed him with every screaming fibre of her wanton body.

He came over her and she folded round him, exulting in his heat and his hardness and his weight. And when he surged into her with primal force the wild burning excitement of his possession drove her out of her senses. He sent her flying with every thrust, until she reached an incredible peak and the expanding ache inside her could no longer be restrained. Then she cried out in ecstasy with him, her body convulsing beneath his before she drowned in the sweet aftermath of satiation.

Encircled in his arms, she felt so safe, so supremely, crazily happy.

'You're always surprising me, *cara*,' César drawled softly above her head, and yet there was something in that light almost lazy intonation which made her tense. 'I really didn't think you'd share a bed with me again.'

Long, elegant fingers turned her flushed face up to his. 'Didn't you? You're like chocolate fudge cake...I can't resist you,' she muttered ruefully.

'The oddest thing is...I rather respected those principles of yours.'

Feeling suddenly very naked and under attack, Dixie pulled out of his arms and rolled over. She was caught in a trap of her own making. It wasn't the pleasure which had seduced her, it was the love, the hungry, overriding need to be as close to him as his skin, and to take what she could for as long as she could.

'And sex on a no strings basis?' César mused in a suspiciously smooth tone bordering on the sardonic. 'I've got to hand it to you. For a female who was a virgin only a few days ago, you learn fast.'

Dixie dug her hot face into the pillow like a hedgehog going into hibernation.

'And possibly it's my incurably suspicious mind at work again, but does your sudden change of heart relate to the fact that now that we've consummated this marriage of ours we can no longer go for an annulment?'

Slowly Dixie raised her head and turned over, dragging the rumpled sheet defensively round herself. 'I don't understand…'

Eyes as keen as silver daggers held hers by sheer force of will. 'We'll have to go for a divorce now. You could make a huge alimony claim.'

Her colour evaporating at that suggestion, her dark blue eyes pained, Dixie simply stuffed her head back in the pillow and turned her back on him.

'No comment?' César probed icily.

So now she was a gold-digger, willing to sacrifice her principles and jump into bed with him purely out of greed! Dixie just sagged, deeply hurt and really angry with him. He could be so stupid when it came to the things that really mattered. He couldn't take anything at superficial value. Didn't he know her at all? How could he have possessed her body with such fiery tenderness while that over-developed brain of his was coming up with such a nasty scenario?

'Does everybody try to rip you off?' she whispered.

'Rarely do I put myself at risk.'

Dixie lifted her head, her dark blue gaze gleaming into chilling, dark, formidable eyes that might have belonged to a stranger. That hurt even more, but she rammed back the pain and tilted her chin. 'Stop worrying. Your bank balance is safe…I'm just using you for sex!'

A stunned light flashed in César's intent stare. 'You didn't say that—'

He looked shocked rigid, and somehow that pleased her. 'Oh, I did. And, blunt as it was, it's really all I've got to say on the subject.'

'You don't mean it…' César released a sudden husky laugh. 'Of course you don't. We're married…you're my wife!'

'You wouldn't accuse your wife of sleeping with you for the sake of money…well, maybe you would,' Dixie conceded, his stock being very low in her eyes at that moment. 'In fact you just did.'

César curved his arms round her rigid, resisting body. 'You changed your mind so suddenly. I have a logical mind. I need to know your motivation.'

'I've just explained that, and will you please let go of me?'

'No.' César planted a kiss at the nape of her neck.

'We're not really married and you know we're not,' she murmured heavily. 'I don't like you saying that we are.'

Instantly, he released her. 'Fine…'

He left her alone then, and she didn't like that either, could feel the stormy tension emanating from him in perceptible waves.

'*And* you owe me an apology,' Dixie muttered miserably.

'I don't apologise to one-night stands,' César breathed witheringly.

The silence stretched and stretched.

'OK,' César ground out tautly. 'I should've reserved comment on a potential alimony claim until it actually happened. Since I asked you to marry me, *and* I asked you to share this bed, my suspicions were unreasonable and unjust.'

There was a definite sense of waiting expectation in the silence which followed that admission of fault, but unfortunately, in relieved receipt of that apology, Dixie just fell asleep, worn out by a very long and emotional day.

Hours later, Dixie lay watching César sleep as the dawn light filtered through the slats of the tall shutters that screened the balcony. Having pushed off the bedding, he lay on his stomach in a relaxed sprawl, his blue-shadowed jawline resting on a brown forearm, ebony lashes gleaming above a slightly flushed cheekbone. He looked younger, less intimidating, incredibly sexy, not an inch of that lean, muscular bronzed body out of condition.

Some time during the night they had collided again, and clung and made love with such frantic intensity she blushed just thinking about it. And she wondered, indeed marvelled that César could desire her as much as he evidently did, and still she couldn't begin to understand it. Sex was clearly very important to César, and hadn't he told her that himself? Bed being the one place he let himself go. Oh, she had already divined that when he had said back in London that she had the kind of shape which kept teenage boys awake and fantasising at night he was talking about himself at that age.

But it didn't mean anything, did it? Physical release, fleeting pleasure on his terms. But she wasn't going to think like that, she scolded herself. She was going to live for the moment.

'Magdalena…my mother, she had tremendous charm and I was very fond of her,' César admitted rather tautly as he lay back against the tumbled pillows like a lithe, bronzed pagan. 'But she was a total airhead. I worried more about her than she did about me.'

'Did you ever meet your father?'

'Once. I was ten. He was curious…that was all,' César admitted without a shade of censure.

'And how did it go?' Dixie prompted.

César grimaced. 'I unnerved him, *cara*. I was a real little nerd at that age, and I had a pretty smart mouth. Yet he left me everything he possessed when he died the following year—probably because I was his only child.'

'So how did you end up going into the family bank?' Dixie asked curiously.

'My father was a playboy all his life, but he expected something more from me,' César conceded with wry amusement. 'He stipulated in his will that I could only inherit his shareholding in Valverde Mercantile if I started at the bank at the bottom and worked my way up.'

'Your first serious girlfriend?' Dixie questioned daringly.

'I was eighteen. I found her in bed with my best friend. I think I can safely say that she was my *only* serious girlfriend.' César leant forward to refill her wine glass.

'You must've been so hurt!' Dixie muttered fiercely.

César smiled at her, a surprisingly tender and amused smile. 'I survived. So tell me about Scott,' he invited.

Dixie blinked. 'What about him?'

'I'm just curious.'

'He likes football and cars. He's twenty-two on his next birthday…' César winced without her noticing as she ran an abstracted fingertip round and round the rim of her glass, wondering why on earth he wanted to hear about Scott. 'He's not a smartass,' she said carefully. 'But he would really love to be called one. Everybody he admires at work seems to be like that, so he wears the same clothes and drives an old Porsche he really can't afford.'

'You're describing a very immature personality.'

'Yes…well, you can't expect him to know everything yet.' Her affection for Scott warmed her smile. 'He's really quite sweet.'

Taking her by surprise, César pulled her into his arms and crushed her soft mouth with fierce, almost angry urgency under his, making her world spin on its axis. 'I'm not sweet…'

Feeling giddy, she scanned the lean strong face above hers with a secretive light in her eyes. She found some of the strangest things sweet when she found them in César. His grizzly bear reaction to her walking away down the beach and getting lost in a book for three hours and totally forgetting about him. His energetic need to be *doing* something every second of the day. His sudden bursts of passion at the most inopportune moments…like when she was in the middle of making a meal or trying to change the bed.

In a week of incredible contentment and happiness, Dixie had learnt a lot about César, and had fallen even more deeply in love with the complex male behind that dark fallen-angel face. He could be so incredibly tender, so honestly affectionate, but always in a hit and run fashion, retreating again fast. Her dog, Spike, had been a bit like that at first, she mused. Full of distrust and unease, afraid to respond to her overtures or express affection.

'What are you thinking about?' César probed, at the wrong moment.

Dixie reddened, knowing he absolutely did not want to know that she had been comparing him to a dog who had been mistreated by a cruel owner in his early years.

'No, don't tell me.' César's bronzed features shuttered as if he had thrown away the key and locked her out.

But she knew what to do when that happened now. She closed her arms round him tight and shut her eyes, as if she was too unobservant to read his signals, and kissed him regardless. He tensed, and then with a hungry driven groan he kissed her back with ravishing need.

'We're leaving the day after tomorrow.' Over an hour later, Dixie was still in César's arms. She was anxious about Jasper's coming surgery, but sad that they had to leave the island.

'No, we're leaving tomorrow.'

'But you said we were flying back on the thirty-first.'

'It'll be the thirty-first in less than five minutes,' César informed her wryly. 'You need a calendar. Somewhere you've lost a day.'

And out of nowhere, as Dixie thought about calendars, something that she had tucked right to the back of her mind struck her. She had always had a twenty-six-day cycle, and today her period should have started, but it hadn't...

So she was late. Perhaps her system had been upset by the change in diet and climate, she told herself feverishly. But what if it wasn't that? What if she had conceived César's baby that very first night?

CHAPTER TEN

'I WANTED to gag Jasper when he started telling us what was in his will!' César confessed, pacing the elegant waiting room like a caged lion and shrugging back his sleeve to consult his slim gold Rolex watch for possibly the fourth time in as many minutes. '*Accidenti!* If I ran a merchant bank the way they run the surgical unit here, I'd be a pauper!'

'Jasper will be fine,' Dixie told him with soothing conviction.

'How can you be so calm?' César demanded, almost accusingly.

'My stepmother was in Intensive Care several times towards the end.'

A veil of dark colour accentuated César's spectacular cheekbones. He breathed in deep and swallowed hard. 'The queen of the gentle put-down, *cara mia*,' he murmured with a wryly apologetic twist of his beautiful mouth. 'I walked smack bang into that one, didn't I?'

'Jasper will come through with flying colours. It's a straightforward procedure.'

César flung himself down on the seat beside her, only to fly upright the instant the door opened. It was the surgeon. His reassuring smile told Dixie all she needed to know, but César talked at length to him. Dixie watched César with her heart in her eyes. He was being very Italian, or was it very Spanish? She smiled. Whichever, he was in a volatile, highly expressive mood, his lean hands moving to illustrate his speech. Not a side of his nature he had ever shown at the bank, where formality and reserve as chilling as ice had always ruled him.

And how would César respond if she chose to tell him that she was carrying his child? Probably with ice. Dixie lost colour, her eyes shadowing with strain. After Jasper had checked into the clinic on the busy outskirts of Granada yesterday, Dixie had mentioned that she had some shopping to do and had slipped away for an hour. She had bought a pregnancy testing kit, and early this morning she had used it. Within minutes the simple test had confirmed that she was pregnant. The shock had hit her hard. Had César not been so worried about Jasper's surgery he might well have questioned the extent of her preoccupation.

How on earth *could* she tell César? He wasn't even aware that there had been cause for concern. She had let him assume that she was taking the contraceptive pill, and since the wedding César had ensured that they took not the smallest risk. Regardless of what she had allowed him to believe, he had still chosen to use protection. Such scrupulous care told Dixie that César was determined not to accidentally father any woman's child.

But it had already been too late. She was carrying César's baby and she didn't feel it was his fault; she felt it was all her fault! And when, as had happened throughout the day, rosy images of a little girl or boy with César's eyes had strayed into Dixie's mind, she felt even guiltier, and more foolish than ever for being so happy with César on the island. In spite of reminding him on their wedding night that their marriage wasn't a real marriage, she had ended up behaving as if it was. Yet their brief but intense relationship was already existing on borrowed time, and within a few weeks would end entirely.

They spent the following day at the clinic, quietly taking turns to sit with Jasper. By that evening, however, César was in an ebullient mood. Being a dire pessimist, having feared the very worst might happen either during surgery or in the crucial recovery period which followed, César's relief at his godfather's continuing steady improvement now knew no bounds.

Back in their luxurious hotel suite, he pulled a full-length gold evening gown out of the closet and dropped it on to the bed. 'Dress up. We're going out to celebrate!'

Had Dixie done her own packing she wouldn't even have had a suitable dress to wear, because it would not have occurred to her that they might go out anywhere special while they were staying in Granada.

Emerging from the shower twenty minutes later, a towel wrapped round his narrow hips, César dropped Dixie's wedding and engagement rings down on the dressing table beside her. 'You leave them absolutely everywhere. Every opportunity you get, you take those rings off and forget about them. Sooner or later they'll be lost or stolen!'

'I'll try to be more careful,' Dixie said in a small voice.

'Sometimes it's like you're trying to make some kind of statement with those rings,' César murmured grittily, but the sight of Dixie rising from the stool, clad only in a highly feminine peach lace bra and diminutive panties, set his mind in what was becoming a very predictable direction.

'*Porca miseria!*' he breathed raggedly. 'You look fantastic!'

As she turned round self-consciously, her cheeks warm, she encountered brilliant dark eyes and felt the wicked weakness and heat he could evoke so easily flood through her trembling body.

'*Dio*...how I want you, *cara*!' César loosened his towel and reached for her in practically the same movement.

He crushed her into the hard, muscular heat of him and she shivered violently, every pulse-point reacting instantaneously. But, for the first time in over a week, a new voice in her head screamed no. Momentarily, she stilled in confusion at that negative prompting, but César's power over her wanton body was greater. Snapping free the bra and casting it aside, he raised his hands to shape her achingly responsive flesh and she was lost, moaning helplessly under his hungry, sensual mouth as he backed her down on to the bed.

It was wilder than it had ever been between them. Raw and sexy and frantically exciting, even shocking in its intensity. He didn't have to wait. She was ready for him. And the instant she felt him inside her she was out of control, reaching a height of intolerable excitement so fast she raked her nails down his back in shaken reaction and he had to smother her scream of release with his mouth.

And then it was over and she was in a complete daze and César was gazing down at her with unconcealed satisfaction. 'It gets better every time,' he said with a very male wolfish grin, sliding off her and then hauling her up into his arms to carry her back into the shower with him.

Only somehow this time she felt embarrassed and ashamed. No longer was it possible to pretend that theirs was a normal relationship. It was really just a casual affair, she told herself. But while she stood under the shower, getting her hair wrecked, knowing it would be wildly curly and unmanageable after a second soaking, an even more disturbing thought occurred to Dixie. It wasn't even an affair. The truth was far less presentable. By settling those debts César had bought her, like a can of peas off a supermarket shelf, and here she was *sleeping* with him as well.

César folded her into a big fleecy towel as if she was a small child. 'I keep on forgetting how new to all this you are,' he drawled softly as he surveyed her evasive eyes and tense mouth. 'But at the same time I like that knowledge. It makes everything so special between us—'

'Does it?'

'Of course it does.' He rested his hands on her taut shoulders, ebony brows drawing together in a frown. 'The last forty-eight hours have been very stressful…we just blew away all that tension in bed and it was electrifying. That's nothing to feel awkward about.'

But Dixie was not in the mood to be comforted. She felt like one of those stress-busting toys businessmen kept on their desks for relaxation. And when César turned away she saw long parallel scratches marring his smooth brown back and just about died a thousand deaths on the spot. She scuttled out of the bathroom to get dressed, feeling hot tears burning the back of her eyes, all her emotions in upheaval at once.

She knew why she was upset. What could be more brutally realistic and impossible to overlook than an unplanned pregnancy which would infuriate the man she loved? Her days of closing her eyes to harsh facts were at end. It wasn't possible to live for the moment with new life growing inside her womb.

César took her to a really fancy restaurant for dinner by candlelight. Dixie wondered out loud why people would want to have to squint at the menu. César requested another candle.

Vintage champagne was brought with a flourish. Dixie asked for mineral water.

César translated the entire menu for her. Then she said she just wanted a salad and played with it.

César had pre-ordered chocolate fudge cake as a surprise. She said she wasn't hungry enough to eat it.

He told her the coffee was a speciality. She told him it tasted metallic and funny.

She left her rings on the sink in the cloakroom. This necessitated a return to the restaurant from the very doors of the nightclub they had been about to enter and twenty-five minutes sitting in a traffic jam. Dixie gave the restaurateur a glum smile of apology and put the rings back on again.

César gave her a brooding look of censure. 'I'm amazed that diamond wasn't stolen.'

'I'm not,' Dixie said, without a shred of remorse for all the inconvenience she'd caused. 'It looks like it fell out of a Christmas cracker!'

César's teeth visibly clenched. 'OK...I've finally got the message. You don't like your engagement ring.'

'It's not mine, it's yours...so what does it matter what I think of it?' Dixie snapped pettishly, shocked at herself, indeed shocked at the way she had been behaving all evening, but quite incapable of controlling the stormy promptings of her own flailing insecurity. And hating César, oh, yes, absolutely hating him as the evening had worn on. Hating him for every smile and every woman who stared at him. Hating him for forgetting about precautions the one time he couldn't afford to forget. Hating him for making her love him and not loving her back...

'*Dio!* What is the matter with you?' César suddenly launched at her halfway back into the limousine. 'Why the hell are you acting like this?'

As she saw his chauffeur swiftly step back in discomfiture, Dixie reddened fiercely and twisted her pounding head away, her true self recoiling from the blunt bewilderment César expressed in spite of his anger.

'You've been like that little girl in the nursery rhyme. You know the one,' César asserted sardonically. 'When she was good, she was very, very good, but when she was bad, she was horrid!'

'I just don't feel like pretending any more.' She wanted to bite down on her tongue but she couldn't; she just couldn't hold the bitterness back.

The silence seemed to scream.

'And what's that cryptic utterance supposed to mean?' César's rich, dark drawl was suddenly cool as ice, and it had been a very long time since he had used that tone with her.

'You're making me feel bad about myself.'

'Using men for sex has its disadvantages,' César incised very drily. 'I thought that was a stupid joke, but now I'm starting to wonder.'

Dixie drew in a breath so deep she was surprised she didn't burst. The bright lights of the city streets flickered in her eyes. 'It's a lot worse than that…'

'Tell me this is a mini-breakdown after all the stress we've had and I'll take a deep breath too and all this bull is going to wash over me while I embrace saint-like restraint!' César shot back at her in a roughened warning.

Dixie desperately wanted to keep quiet, but she couldn't. Now all those feelings had foamed up inside her, she had to let them out. 'What we've got is very sordid—'

'I didn't hear that.'

'You bought the right to tell me what to do when you paid those debts. You said that yourself,' Dixie reminded him shakily. 'And I could just about live with that if we hadn't ended up in bed—'

'When we made that deal there was nothing between us. We've gone way beyond that level since then!'

'Well, I still really hate you for what you've done to me!' Dixie told him wildly. But even as she slung those bitter words she knew that she wanted him to pull her into his arms and tell her she was talking rubbish and make her feel safe again, not just sit there like an insensitive stone watching her tear herself apart!

'OK.' César stared at her, lean, strong face ferociously taut, eyes a bright lambent silver as unreadable as a mirror, and then he lifted the phone to communicate with his chauffeur. Minutes later, the limo drew out of the traffic and purred in at the front of their hotel.

'I'll see you tomorrow at the clinic,' César breathed without inflection, and a moment later the passenger door beside Dixie opened for her to get out.

'*Tomorrow?* Where are you going?' she demanded helplessly.

'I don't think that's anything which need concern you now.'

It had never once occurred to Dixie that César might just walk out on her and the argument she had begun. It felt like the cruellest kind of punishment. Appalled into silence, she climbed out and watched the limo pull back into the flow of traffic.

She already knew she had made a dreadful mistake. She had wrecked the relationship they did have. Getting a grip on her wildly fluctuating emotions, she sat up waiting for César to come back. At that point she was absolutely convinced that in spite of what he had said he would return to the hotel. But at three in the morning she went to bed and fell into an uneasy doze, only to wake up still alone at dawn, and feel very scared.

He had probably just gone back to the hacienda for the night. It was only an hour's drive away, she reminded herself. They were only in a hotel because it was more convenient while they were spending so much time with Jasper.

Experiencing a very real need to talk to someone about the mess she had made of things, Dixie toyed with the idea of ringing Petra, where she was staying on the coast. But the nagging awareness that confiding in her stepsister on her wedding day had given her nothing but grief held her back. And César, who wouldn't dream of confiding anything private in anybody, even under torture, would be furious if she was indiscreet.

So Dixie buttoned up her desire to unburden herself, but ended up succumbing to the temptation to ring Scott for another chat, just to fill in the time until she could go to the clinic and sit with Jasper. Scott was much more cheerful. He had been told that he would be free to return to London within a fortnight. Emboldened by that news, he had ventured out to explore New York, but only got as far as the car showrooms. He spent most of the call talking at length about a car he had fallen in love with.

More clued up about Corvettes than she had ever wanted to be, but relieved Scott was happier, Dixie took a taxi to the clinic around ten. It was distinctly humiliating to arrive with Jasper and discover that although César had not been in touch with her he had already sent a message to his godfather. It did not occur to her that she had stayed on the phone to New York for well over an hour because she hadn't the slightest idea that the call had actually lasted that long.

'Such a shame that you and César have to be separated so soon after the wedding,' Jasper sighed with sympathy.

'Sorry?' Dixie prompted uncertainly.

'This stockmarket crisis…César having to rush back to London,' Jasper filled in gloomily. 'Said he'd call in on the way to the airport. You should go with him. You shouldn't be sitting about here with me.'

Stockmarket crisis? What stockmarket crisis? César was rushing back to London? In receipt of that devastating news, it was a challenge to summon up a sunny reproving smile, but Dixie managed it because she cared so much about the old man anxiously watching for her reaction. 'I *love* sitting about here with you!'

Jasper's forlorn look evaporated. 'I expect César will be far too busy to spend time with you over the next few days anyway,' he conceded. 'He's a terrible workaholic.'

César was returning to London. César was leaving her behind in Spain, just the way it had always been planned, Dixie reminded herself numbly. César had already been away from Valverde Mercantile for more than two weeks.

Soon Jasper would be able to go home to convalesce, and she would stay on to keep him company and ensure he didn't try to do too much too soon.

She chatted to Jasper, and only when the sound of answering silence finally penetrated did she appreciate that he had fallen asleep. She couldn't even recall what she had been talking about. Feeling the need to stretch her legs, she slipped out of the room, only to stop dead again.

César was striding down the corridor towards her. In a fabulous light grey pinstripe business suit teamed with a white shirt and silver silk tie, he was no longer the relaxed and smiling male she had come to expect. As he drew to a halt a couple of feet from her he looked cold, distant and unbelievably intimidating.

Meeting those chilling dark deep-set eyes, she felt as she had that very first day she had gone into his office, to be faced with the computer print-out listing Petra's debts. The shock of that realisation made Dixie shiver in disbelief. It was as if everything that had happened between them since then only existed in her own imagination.

'Jasper's asleep,' she muttered unevenly.

'He needs all the rest he can get. I'll call him this evening.'

Dixie breathed in deep and braced herself to say what she knew needed to be said. 'César, I'm really sorry about the way I acted last night—'

'Forget it,' César cut in with dismissive, deflating cool.

Her tension screamed up another notch. It was as if a terrifying wall of impenetrable glass separated him from her. It was as if they had never made love, never laughed together, never shared anything. 'I *can't*…I didn't mean it when I said I hate—'

'I don't want to talk about this.' He was cold as ice, his impatience unhidden.

Involuntarily, Dixie's eyes just filled with tears.

With a soft, succinct expletive, César splayed a hand over her spine to press her another few yards down the corridor into the empty waiting room. He didn't close the door, though. As he walked over to the window a nurse walked past, her footsteps an audible reminder that they didn't have privacy. Then Dixie sensed that César didn't want privacy, didn't want to speak to her in depth, didn't want to be with her one second more than he had to be. The completeness of that rejection savaged her like a physical blow.

And, suddenly feeling dizzy, she sank heavily down into a chair. 'You're dumping me…' She hadn't meant to say that, hadn't even thought of saying that, but somehow that was what emerged from her bloodless lips.

Ferocious tension radiated from every inch of César's rigid back view. He dug coiled fists into the pockets of his well-cut trousers, tightening the fine fabric over his long powerful thighs, but he didn't turn round and he didn't respond.

'Where did you go last night?' Dixie whispered shakily, desperate to talk just to keep him with her, because her whole world felt as if it was shattering around her.

'The beach.'

'Wh-what beach?' she stammered, completely thrown by that admission, as Granada was a long drive from the coast.

'A beach...OK? What does it matter *where* I went?' César gritted in a driven undertone.

'I was worried about you...you told me once not to do that.' Dixie recalled in a sick daze.

'I've settled the hotel bill.' César half turned towards her and then swung back to the window again, but not before she had seen the fierce tautening of his strong profile. 'You'll be more comfortable staying at the hacienda. Jasper's chauffeur will run you back and forth. In a couple of weeks you can come back to London. We'll sort out the rest then.'

If there was a right moment to tell César that she was carrying his baby, Dixie acknowledged painfully, this was definitely not it, here where they could be interrupted at any time or overheard.

César finally spun round. He treated her to a glittering diamond-hard appraisal, not a revealing muscle moving on his darkly handsome face. Then, slowly elbowing back his superbly tailored jacket, he removed something from the inner pocket. 'You might as well have *this*...' He tossed the tiny item with studied casualness down on her lap. 'I'm never going to give it to anybody else.'

In complete astonishment, Dixie gazed down at the exquisite ruby ring, the sunlight gleaming over the beautiful jewel's rich gleaming density of colour.

'Throughout this whole thing you've been really great.' César hovered uneasily halfway towards the open door, like a male being painfully pulled in two different directions, lines of deep strain engraved between his nose and compressed mouth, brilliant eyes screened. 'I should've told you that first...but I wasn't in the mood. You should sell that ring. Scott may not know it yet, but keeping you in washing machines will probably be more of a challenge than keeping a Porsche on the road!'

Scott? Why was César suddenly talking about Scott? Dixie's brain refused to function. Why was he behaving so unnaturally? Was he reminding her about Scott in the hope that she would pick up on that prompting and stop being so embarrassingly emotional?

'Yes,' Dixie muttered flatly. 'But it won't be a Porsche. It'll be a Corvette.'

'Sorry, am I interrupting?' a bright familiar female voice exclaimed from the doorway.

Dixie's head flew up and she gaped, utterly taken aback by the sight of her stepsister standing there, her sleek brown torso and endless long legs on show in a white lace top and brief flirty skirt. 'Petra…?' she breathed in bewilderment.

'I thought César was going to bring you down to the car to see me, but I got fed up waiting.' Petra flicked back her stunning golden mane of hair, a distinctly petulant look on her lovely face. 'I feel like I've spent the whole morning in that blasted car *waiting*!'

César frowned at Dixie. 'Sorry, I forgot to mention that your sister had decided to fly back to London with me.'

'Forgot?' Petra repeated thinly, but then she plastered a wide, bright smile on her lips and shrugged. 'This guy is just so bad for my ego!'

Dixie just looked through the two of them, refusing to focus on either as she struggled valiantly to conceal the most sick sense of betrayal. So, César had gone to the beach. And who had been staying by that beach? She understood now, wished she didn't. So much for his impressively stated dislike of Petra! Last night César had walked away from her and deliberately sought out her beautiful stepsister's company.

'It's time I got back to Jasper.' Pale as death, Dixie scrambled upright, eager to escape both her companions. 'Have a good trip back to London!'

'Dixie…?' Halfway down the corridor César caught up with her, but he only succeeded in halting her by catching hold of her hand.

Unwillingly, Dixie spun back. *'What?'* she demanded baldly.

César gazed down at her with charged dark eyes, and then very slowly let go of her hand again. 'Nothing…nothing at all!' he breathed fiercely, and strode away.

Dixie leant back against the wall until she had stopped trembling, and as soon as he was out of sight dived into the cloakroom to be ingloriously and horribly sick.

CHAPTER ELEVEN

THREE weeks later, Dixie arrived back in London.

Every evening for those three weeks César had phoned her. After she had given her daily bulletin on Jasper, César had then questioned her in astonishing detail about what she did every day, right down to what she was reading. And every evening she had just talked and talked about nothing in particular, just so that she could keep on hearing the sound of that rich, dark drawl. Not once had either of them referred to their marriage, their once intimate relationship, or the divorce that now had to be on the cards.

Indeed, César's constant calls had utterly bewildered Dixie, until she had belatedly worked out that he was behaving exactly as Jasper would expect a newly married husband to behave when he was separated from his wife. Naturally there would be no necessity for such pretences once she was back in London.

Dixie was a complete bag of nerves by the time César's chauffeur met her off her flight. She hadn't been sleeping well, and keeping up a sunny façade for Jasper had been a strain. And three long endless weeks away from César's enervating presence had forced her to face too many depressing realities.

What they had briefly shared was over. For César, it had been a casual sexual affair. For her, it had been the most wonderful but ultimately the most traumatic experience of her life. And right now she still felt that she was never, ever going to recover. She had known César had a very low tolerance for the kind of scene she had thrown that night in Granada, but she still felt that even he could have practised sufficient consideration not to make it obvious that he was planning to replace her with her own stepsister.

But she was equally aware that she couldn't afford to wallow in her squashed ego or her misery. She was pregnant. She was broke. She was unemployed. To save face she would very much have liked to vanish out of César's life with a cheery smile, but as matters now stood that wasn't an option open to her. It was time she told César about the baby. She had been tempted to just blurt the news out on the phone, but had decided that that would be the coward's way out.

It was afternoon when Dixie trekked wearily in the chauffeur's wake towards the limousine parked outside the airport. She wasn't expecting to have to face César before evening. So when the passenger door suddenly opened and César climbed gracefully out she was completely unprepared, and an expression of unconcealed dismay froze her face.

And that dismay merely concealed a whole host of humiliating and all too personal reactions. César looked so impossibly gorgeous. Black hair gleaming in the sunshine, stunning dark eyes just zooming in on her susceptible heart and stealing it back again. Feeling the tarmac literally rock beneath her feet, Dixie came to a halt, just staring endlessly at him, wondering with a deep sense of injustice why he had to look so fantastically sexy and exotic in an incredibly elegant cream designer suit. And here she was, a make-up-free zone, hair curling and wearing the first outfit she had pulled out of the wardrobe.

'I'd have met you off the plane, but Spike doesn't like being left alone in the car...' César began tautly.

'S-Spike?'

An agonised whine sounded from the back seat. César bent down and reached in and emerged with Spike, his little short legs pedalling in the air with excitement, pleading brown eyes prominent.

Dixie just dived at Spike. Reaching him out of César's arms, she scrambled into the car to take part in an ecstatic reunion with her pet. By the time Spike had been restored to order the limo was a long way from the airport, and Dixie was grateful for the distraction.

'I can't believe he came with you.' Dixie watched as Spike arranged himself between them, like a dog trying to stretch himself to three times his natural length so that he could be in contact with both. 'My goodness, he's not the slightest bit scared of you!'

Spike made that comment somewhat redundant by giving Dixie's hand an apologetic lick, then squirming round and sneaking in the most grovelling fashion imaginable across the back seat to settle down beside César and look up at him with worshipping eyes.

'He's quite friendly,' César conceded in modest understatement, stroking Spike's tufty ears and reducing the Jack Russell to a mindless heap of bliss.

'I just never thought…I mean, he was so *terrified* of men!' With difficulty, Dixie mastered her astonishment. 'It took me ages to win his trust, but obviously you have the magic touch…only…' She bit her lip anxiously. 'He's going to be very upset if he loses you now.'

'Yes, I feel it could really traumatise him,' César agreed reflectively. 'You'll have to try to detach him from me by easy stages.'

'Yes, of course.'

'I shouldn't think you'll be able to consider moving out of my house in the near future,' César sighed.

Dixie continued to survey Spike with wondering eyes. Welded to César's thigh, he was the very picture of intense doggy devotion. 'I guess not…'

A slow smile nudged at the corners of César's once tense lip-line. 'I have to confess I've spoilt him.'

'He needed spoiling.'

Silence fell. Dixie watched Spike as though her life depended on it. He was a great ice-breaker, she thought ruefully. And she couldn't help but be touched to see César being so kind to her distinctly scruffy little pet. She had really been dreading seeing César again after that emotionally devastating final meeting at the clinic. Unfortunately even Spike wasn't likely to be much use as a diversion once she told César what she had to tell him…

'When we get back to the house,' Dixie began, deciding that César deserved some warning of what was coming his way, 'we'll have to talk. I'm afraid I've got something really serious and shocking—well, *very* shocking to confess, and you're not going to be very happy about it… In fact, I think you're likely to be really annoyed, and I want to say now in advance that that is understandable—'

'Scott flew out to Spain and you sneaked out and slept with him…' César slotted in rawly.

Dixie's lashes fluttered up on incredulous dark blue eyes. She couldn't have responded to such an outrageous suggestion had her life depended on it.

'*Madre di Dio*...anything of that nature, keep it to yourself, because "annoyed" won't cover it. I'll *kill* him!' César swore in a voice that fractured between visibly clenched teeth.

'What's the matter with you? Have you been drinking...or something?' Dixie enquired tautly.

'No, but I badly need a large shot of alcohol,' César confided jaggedly as he leant forward and wrenched open the drinks cabinet.

'Scott has not been in Spain.' Hot, mortified colour now bloomed in Dixie's cheeks. 'And I can't imagine why you think he would've been, or that I would do what you suggested. Perhaps you think I behaved in a rather impulsive fashion with you, but believe me, I've learnt my lesson.'

César thrust shut the drinks cabinet without succumbing to temptation. He drew in a deep, steadying breath. 'I had nerves of steel until I met you.'

'I was just trying to prepare you for what I have to tell you,' Dixie muttered ruefully.

'Relax. I'm cool as ice,' César informed her with glittering dark eyes of probing enquiry that made it very hard for her to breathe. 'Battle-hardened, unshockable, and ready to cope with anything you want to throw at me.'

The limo drew up outside the house. Dixie smiled at Fisher as he opened the imposing front door.

'Welcome home, Mrs Valverde,' the butler said with immense warmth.

'Oh, no, who told you we were married?' Dixie gasped in dismay, looking worriedly at César. 'It's a really big secret!'

'It's all round the bank too,' César told her apologetically.

Dixie's eyes got even bigger. 'Bruce didn't keep quiet? Oh, how awful for you, César!'

'I'm bearing up surprisingly well. And I wish I could tell you that it was a seven-day wonder, but it's a story set to run and run, and that in itself has created certain problems you may not have foreseen,' César confided, curving a determined arm over her spine and walking her fast towards his study, Spike at their heels.

'Problems?'

'Wedding presents, invitations out as a couple—'

'*Wedding* presents?' Dixie exclaimed in horror.

César slammed shut the door, leant back against it with squared shoulders and breathed. 'OK...give me the really serious, very shocking bad news. Don't keep me in suspense...'

Dazed by the revelation that their marriage was now a matter of public knowledge, and feeling rather light-headed from the effects of stress and tiredness, Dixie surveyed César with open misery.

'I just wish I hadn't been foolish enough to let you think what I let you think... You see, I'm not and I've never been taking the contraceptive pill,' she admitted tightly, and waited for César to leap to the obvious conclusion.

His lush black lashes dropped very low over his fiercely intent eyes. 'What's that got to do with anything?'

A wave of dizziness ran over Dixie. She swayed slightly.

'You've gone white!' Striding forward on that exclamation, César steadied her with two careful hands and backed her down gently on to a leather couch.

'I'm pregnant...' Dixie told him flatly as he dropped down on a level with her.

'Pregnant,' César repeated, as if he had never heard the word before.

'That night Jasper collapsed...' Dixie added in a helpful whisper, wondering when the awful truth was going to sink in.

'You're pregnant...' César's eyes suddenly silvered and flashed. 'All of a sudden I feel...almost dizzy,' he completed, not quite levelly.

Dixie just couldn't bear to watch his next reaction. She bowed her head over her tightly clasped hands and waited for the storm to break. In the circumstances, he would have to be superhuman not to lament such bad luck.

'You've got my baby inside you…' César framed with audible difficulty, his dark deep drawl roughening.

'After just that one time,' Dixie sighed shakily.

César unlaced her fingers with gentle force and wound them into his palms. '*Dio*…just that one time, *cara mia*,' he swore in the strangest tone.

'You're very shocked. I don't blame you. You were so careful every other time…' Her voice trailed away in embarrassment.

'The hand of fate is definitely operating here,' César remarked, sounding buoyant in what she could only assume to be his evident determination not to hurt her feelings or cause offence in any way. 'But I'm much inclined to think this is only what you call a storm in a teacup—'

'A storm in a teacup?' Dixie parroted in disbelief.

'Obviously you're not looking on the bright side,' César censured silkily. 'We're married—not that anyone would guess that by the ringless state of your hands.'

'I took the rings off as soon as I said goodbye to Jasper. I thought our marriage was to stay a secret,' she explained, mystified by the turn the conversation had taken, still apprehensively fearing a more painful response to the revelation that she had conceived.

Vaulting upright, César bent down and lifted her slowly into his arms. 'You need to lie down. You're very tired.'

'We need to talk about this now.'

'When you're more comfortable.'

Supporting her with one powerful arm, César opened the door and strode across the hall to mount the stairs. 'This isn't where I sleep,' she protested.

'It's just not the done thing to keep your wife in the servants' quarters.'

'I was very comfortable there…I really don't want to intrude,' Dixie said miserably. 'You've got marvellous self-discipline, haven't you? You still haven't said one thing that I thought you would say.'

'It's a mistake to try and second-guess me. And I don't want to be discouraging, but because your mind works on a different plane from mine you don't read me very well,' César declared ruefully.

He settled her down on a magnificent canopied bed in a spacious room that had a distinctly masculine decor of burgundy and dark green. Several other doors led off from it. It was a truly massive house. Slipping off her shoes, he helped her out of her light jacket, pausing with amusement to scrutinise the price label still attached to the garment.

'So, say what you have to say,' Dixie urged anxiously.

'After you've had a nap, *cara*.' César sank down on the side of the bed, lean bronzed features arranged in an expression of unbelievable calm. 'You came close to fainting downstairs and you're still very pale. We've got plenty of time to talk.'

Dixie pushed her face into a pillow. 'Stop being nice,' she pleaded in a pained voice. 'It just makes me feel more of a nuisance. I know you don't really feel nice...it's just you hide your true feelings better than I do.'

César smoothed one of her curls down, watched it spring back rebelliously and smiled. 'Go to sleep,' he murmured softly. 'If it's any consolation, I used to think I could read you like a book, and then I discovered that there's nothing logical about the way you think. It's all gut reaction and impulses with you, thrills and spills...'

'Not true,' she mumbled, just loving him being there, too exhausted even to despise herself for being that weak. She might as well enjoy it, she thought. He wouldn't be there for much longer.

Dixie slept until almost seven that evening. When she wakened, she went for a shower and thought about César. He had been really kind. Why had she expected anything else? He was too sophisticated and too self-disciplined to react like a scared teenager trying to escape his responsibilities. But would kindness ultimately prove to be any easier to bear?

Fisher came to the door to inform her that dinner would be served at eight. She put on an elegant black sleeveless dress. She had worn it on the island, but the new fullness of her breasts gave the dress a tighter fit. Already her body was changing shape, an ever-present reminder of the tiny life forming inside her.

In the formal dining room, Fisher had set out magnificent silver candelabra and the very best china and crystal. Poor Fisher, Dixie reflected ruefully. He couldn't have a clue how inappropriate the romantic approach was for this particular occasion.

César joined her in the doorway. She turned. Tall, dark and devastatingly attractive, he made her outrageously aware of her own femininity.

'Do you think you can tolerate candlelight for one meal?' César enquired lazily.

Recalling that dreadful evening in Granada, Dixie went pink. 'I was really awful that night, wasn't I?' she groaned. 'I'd just found out I was pregnant and I went into a sort of tailspin—'

César frowned in surprise. 'You knew about the baby that far back?'

Dixie nodded.

'No wonder you were upset,' César settled her down into her chair.

Fisher served their meal. It was delicious, and she was hungry, but she couldn't have said what she ate. Afterwards, they had coffee in the drawing room, and her tension started to rocket again.

'Can we get the rest of this discussion over with?' Dixie asked, rising restively from her seat and beginning to wander aimlessly round the room. 'I don't understand how you can just make conversation as if there's nothing wrong!'

Slumbrous dark eyes rested on her. 'The obvious answer to that is that as far as I'm concerned there *is* nothing wrong. I want this baby,' César countered with incredible cool.

Dixie didn't see that that was necessarily the slightest bit obvious. 'But it was an accident—'

'No, and don't ever use that expression again.' César's mouth twisted as he moved forward to steady a tall lamp which she had brushed past. 'Take it from one who knows, tiny babies grow into adolescents who do not want to live with the news that they are the result of an accidental lapse in birth control!'

Dixie flushed and backed into a chair before setting off in another direction. 'I know that, but—'

'I can't believe that you would want a termination.'

'I don't.' Dixie stiffened defensively. 'But I thought you might.'

'That's not something I need to think about. My father tried to deprive me of the right to be born,' César reminded her with wry distaste. 'I could never feel like that about my own child. I don't just *want* our baby, I also intend to be a good father right from the start.'

Both those sweeping statements of intent left Dixie bereft of breath. Not once had she even hoped for that level of acceptance or commitment from César. 'That'll be difficult when we're living apart...divorced, I mean,' she finally pointed out awkwardly, coming to a halt as she met with another obstacle.

Helpfully, César removed the entire jardinière from her path. 'I'm afraid this is where *you* have to be very brave and self-sacrificing, *cara mia*.' He surveyed her with glittering dark eyes full of expectation.

'I don't understand...'

César spread fluidly expressive hands in a gesture of finality. 'It's goodbye to Scott time.'

'Goodbye to Scott?' Dixie marvelled at the way poor Scott seemed to intrude in all sorts of places where he didn't belong.

'If we both want to do what is best for our child, we won't even consider getting a divorce now,' César asserted with complete conviction, watching her turn in little circles in the centre of the room.

Wildly disconcerted by that announcement, and giddy at the mere thought of it, Dixie breathed, 'But—'

'So we stay together, but Scott's *out* of our lives,' César stressed tautly. 'You have to accept that.'

'But Scott's just a friend—'

'You spent one hour and forty-two minutes on the phone to New York from our hotel in Granada,' César cited in a low-pitched growl of censure, making no move to protect her from stubbing her toe on the edge of the marble hearth. 'That was at least one hour and thirty minutes of what I call excessive friendship!'

Dixie studied him wide-eyed and then stumbled over the hearth. She righted herself with a bracing hand on the superb fireplace and slowly shook her head. 'Oh, my goodness…was I really on the phone that long? How on earth do you *know* that?'

'I paid the hotel bill before I came to the clinic,' César reminded her grittily.

He really was obsessed with Scott. She couldn't think how she had failed to notice that before. And he was genuinely angry that she had chatted that long to Scott on the phone. Was he jealous? Jealous of Scott? And being Dixie, in the grip of an astounding idea, she instantly asked him outright.

Dark colour accentuated César's fantastic cheekbones, lashes sweeping down on bright slivers of silvered outrage. '*Porca miseria!* Don't be ridiculous!'

Dixie flushed, and now saw no reason to add that she had long since got over her conviction that Scott was ever likely to be anything other than a friend. 'Sorry. I just—'

As she wandered back near the lamp table, César put his hands on her slight shoulders and directed her down on to a sofa. 'You're making me dizzy. Stay put,' he instructed. 'All I am saying is that there is only room for two people in this marriage. You and I.'

'What about Petra?' Dixie almost whispered, knotting her fingers together.

Strong face clenching, his expressive mouth curled. 'I can put up with her in small doses, but if you could persuade her that covering up a little more flesh would make her look less like a hooker, I'd be grateful.'

Stunned by that sardonic response, Dixie studied him fixedly from below her lashes. 'But you went to see Petra the night you left me at the hotel—'

'No, I did not go to see her. I ran into her…to be exact, she ran into me the following morning,' César contradicted with careful clarity, seemingly quite unaware of Dixie's extreme tension. 'I do own the block of apartments she was staying in. I used one myself that night. Petra saw the limo, invited herself over for breakfast and expressed a desire to return to London with me. I could hardly refuse.'

César drew a perfectly possible scenario. Yet no matter how badly Dixie wanted to believe him, newly learnt cynicism assailed her. César was so clever. Would César tell her a truth that would hurt her now that he was talking about staying married to her? If he had been attracted to her stepsister, if he had followed through on that attraction, it would be very foolish of him to confess it now and drive an uneasy wedge between Dixie and Petra.

All Dixie knew was that she still couldn't quite follow what had been going on with César, either that night or the following morning. He had come to the clinic armed with a fabulous ruby ring as a kind of goodbye gift. Petra had been unusually brittle and awkward, exactly as she might have behaved had she got 'close' to Dixie's supposed temporary husband.

'You created a problem there,' César drawled, as if he could read her mind. 'You should never have told Petra that our marriage was a fake.'

Dixie stiffened. Her second mistake had been stopping short of complete honesty. Had she confided that she and César were rather more than platonic partners, her stepsister would surely never have admitted or acted on her interest in him. So if anything *had* happened between César and Petra that night on the coast it was partly her own fault, not least for saying all those ghastly things about their relationship and tearing it apart.

'Did she tell you where she'd be staying in London?' Dixie asked uncomfortably.

'No, just that she'd be with a friend.'

'I'm sure she'll be in touch soon.'

'I shouldn't think we've seen the last of her,' César remarked quietly.

Dixie's thoughts were on her stepsister. It made her unhappy to acknowledge that the wedge between herself and Petra already existed, in the form of her own insecurity. And she knew then that she would have to talk to Petra before she could put those secret and undoubtedly quite foolish fears away.

As soon as Dixie had decided that, she was then free to appreciate how very happy she actually was. There wasn't going to be a divorce. César was determined that their child should have the stable background and support he himself had been denied. A little of her happiness ebbed on her next acknowledgement: if she hadn't been pregnant, César would have been discussing their divorce right now.

'I'm not sure you could cope with being married to me for years and years,' Dixie remarked ruefully.

César tensed. 'Why not?'

'You get bored awfully easy.' All her doubts showed in her eyes.

'How could I possibly get bored with you? I never know what you're about to spring on me from one minute to the next!'

'The trouble is, I also know you're not very good at being faithful.'

'Try me! *Dios mio*,' César rhymed, visibly shaking at having that thrown in his teeth. 'You seem so soft and trusting, but when it comes to me you're really tough and suspicious!'

Dixie thought about that and decided it was very true. 'You wouldn't respect anything else,' she pointed out helplessly.

'Tell me, were you like this with Scott?'

'No. He's not very clever and ruthless—'

'I forgot…he was really sweet,' César breathed with derisive bite.

Fisher knocked on the door to mention an urgent call.

After waiting fifteen minutes, and deciding that César might well be absolute ages, Dixie walked back upstairs at a sedate pace. With a gentle hand she shut the bedroom door. Then she took an undignified leap on to the wellsprung bed, punched the pillows with exuberant energy, rolled over again to kick off her shoes and gasped, 'Yes...yes...*yes!*'

The door that led into the connecting sitting room was ajar. Slowly it spread wide to frame César. Lounging back against the doorjamb, an unholy grin slashing his dark features as he absorbed Dixie's paralysed expression of appalled chagrin, he cast aside the cordless phone in his hand.

'So, I must be pretty good at doing something, *cara mia,*' César remarked with sexy sibilant softness. 'Downstairs, I would never have credited that you had the slightest enthusiasm for staying married to me. But here you are celebrating all by yourself. Fancy that.'

'I...I—'

César shimmied his shoulders fluidly out of his jacket and pitched it on a nearby chair. Tugging loose his tie, he surveyed her widening eyes and the colour building in her cheeks.

'Yes, now you *know* when I want you!' César carolled with satisfaction. 'That has to be a step in the right direction.'

And Dixie just couldn't control her response to the atavistic leap of boundless excitement tearing through her. He came down beside her on the bed with a brilliant smile that tore her heart from its moorings. Heat pooled deep inside her and made her tremble, and yet beyond that she was conscious of the most powerful ache of tenderness. Gosh, he just looked so really happy, even happier than he had been on the island. The first thing she did was hug him tight, straining against him as the last of her tension drained away in the circle of his arms.

'I've really missed you...' he groaned raggedly.

In bed, she translated.

'I've even been thinking about you when I'm at the bank,' he confessed.

Thinking about the frustrating emptiness of the bed, she translated.

He curved his fingers to her cheekbones and kissed her breathless, so much hungry need in his stunning dark eyes she couldn't stop staring, still marvelling at the miracle which had made this elegant, cool, often cold guy seemingly burn with endless desire for her uncool and never elegant self.

'I got used to you being there...now you're here,' he completed, with a wealth of relief in his roughened intonation.

Back in the bed, she translated, but she ached with love for him, and told herself she wasn't going to want any more than he was able to give her. And tomorrow she would put on the ruby ring. Bit of a joke, that, she conceded. César had given her a ring that symbolised *her* passionate love for *him*, just because rubies were the only jewels she had seemed to have no reservations about...

'So I want to see Scott one last time,' Dixie concluded in the simmering silence. One glorious week had passed since her return to London, and this was their first difference of opinion.

'No,' César said flatly.

'Just to explain that I've got married and that that's why I haven't been in touch,' Dixie repeated for the second time.

'I don't want you anywhere near him. I think that's perfectly reasonable,' César drawled.

'Well, I don't,' Dixie muttered ruefully. 'I don't think it's reasonable at all. Nor do I think that you should behave as if I need your permission.'

'You're my wife,' César breathed chillingly, like a domestic tyrant. 'You should *care* about what I think.'

These days Dixie wasn't as easily chilled as she had once been. 'It's not like Scott's an ex-boyfriend or anything. I would understand if you were jealous—'

'I'm *not* jealous!' César gritted with predictable ferocity. 'Jealousy would imply that I regard him as a threat. Why would I consider an immature twenty-two-year-old car fanatic a threat?'

'I used to imagine I was in love with Scott, but I got over that ages ago,' Dixie remarked with studious casualness.

The silence hung there, throbbing with undertones.

'OK.' César flung the *Financial Times* down across the breakfast table and stood up. 'You can meet him somewhere public for an hour.'

'I'll call him today...' Dixie returned to her book and her coffee with an aura of complete tranquillity.

César reached the door at an unusually slow pace, and then swung back. 'I could come too,' he suggested abruptly.

Without lifting her head, Dixie muttered, 'Not much point you meeting him now. Anyway, he'd be so in awe of someone like you he wouldn't be able to relax.'

'I should hate to be a third wheel.'

Dixie laughed at that idea, knowing that César would simply take over.

'Why don't you ring Scott next week, when Jasper's here?' César suggested then, as he hovered by the door. 'I'm sure Jasper would love to meet him.'

'No, I don't want to leave it that long.' Dixie looked up and gave him a sunny smile, finally registering that he was about to leave. 'Will you be home for lunch?'

The brooding look on his lean bronzed face evaporated like magic. 'I'd really love to, but lunch at home exhausts me.'

Dixie coloured.

'Actually, I'm down for a very boring diplomatic do at lunchtime today...I'd much rather be with you,' César murmured, still lingering while she went back to her book.

In bed, she was thinking. Typical. But she warmed up inside with the wonderful safe feeling she was beginning to experience around César now. Sexual desire might have got him involved with her in the first place, but he was turning out to be so surprisingly wonderful in other ways.

According to Fisher, César had gone to fantastic lengths to win Spike's affection. Spike had been lured from his various hiding places with chocolate drops, doggy bones, choice treats from the dining table and toys. With a patience and a determination that had quite dumbfounded his butler, César had inched and pushed his way into Spike's scared little heart. And Dixie was incredibly touched that a male who had never had a pet in his life had made such a big effort. Initially he could only have done it to please her, but now he had been doubly rewarded by Spike's devotion.

Then there was the custom-built pond her goldfish now rejoiced in. César the fish hadn't eaten his companion, Milly, and they swam around together occasionally now. It would be too much to call them inseparable, but who knew what the future might hold?

Indeed, the only thing that troubled Dixie was that César hadn't yet offered to try to help her locate Petra. She still didn't know where her stepsister was staying. She had thrown out loads of hints, but either César hadn't picked up on them or he preferred that her stepsister remain out of touch. And Dixie had worked out that that was either because he genuinely couldn't stand Petra or because possibly something *had* happened between them which he didn't want Dixie to find out about...

But that was the only current cloud on Dixie's horizon. Next week, when Jasper arrived to spend the rest of the summer with them, they were having a belated wedding reception with five hundred guests. Dixie felt married now. Every time she woke up in the morning in César's arms she felt jubilant. It was the little things that mattered. The way he phoned her from the bank on what sometimes seemed the slimmest pretext. The way he had laughed at the sight of Spike trying to drag a bone nearly as big as himself upstairs. The way he talked about the baby, as if he or she was already here and part of their lives.

Dixie rang Scott at work mid-morning and told him she had got married. He reacted as if he was really shocked, and was surprisingly keen to make an arrangement to meet up with her that evening. She had rather thought he mightn't want to bother.

And then, at lunchtime, without the smallest warning, Dixie's world fell apart again. Bruce Gregory phoned to ask her where César was lunching.

She frowned in surprise. 'He mentioned an embassy thing—'

'No, he cancelled that to meet with your stepsister, and he must have his mobile switched off. I assumed he'd be back with you, at the house, but Fisher said not. So, do you know where they are?' Bruce prompted hopefully, quite unconscious of the bombshell he had dropped. 'The chairman of the Osana Corporation wants to speak to César urgently.'

Dixie's lips moved to frame conventional words before she could find her actual voice. 'I'm sorry, I didn't pick up on where they were planning to go.'

Bruce rang off, leaving Dixie sitting there in shock. César was with Petra? All this time César had known where her stepsister was? Well, obviously he had, if he was lunching with her! And yet he hadn't mentioned it to Dixie, even when he knew how worried she was that Petra hadn't been in touch?

Dear heaven, were they having an affair? If Dixie hadn't conceived, their marriage would have been over now. Yet César hadn't been acting like a male trapped in a marriage he didn't want! Or had he been? Had she just been too dumb and too much in love to see the obvious? Although if César was involved with Petra, why was he dragging Dixie off to bed early every night?

Half an hour later, Fisher opened the door of the drawing room. 'Miss Sinclair, madam.'

And before Dixie could even catch her breath, Petra erupted into the room, tear-stained and almost hysterical.

'I've done something dreadful, and you're going to hate me, but you're the only person who can help me!' her stepsister gasped before Fisher even got the door closed behind her.

'Help you?' Dixie was already rising from her seat.

'I made an awful mistake. I tried to blackmail César!' Petra ran a trembling berringed hand through her tumbled blonde tresses and groaned. 'How could you marry a ruthless bastard like that, Dixie?'

Dixie had slumped heavily back into her seat. Blackmail? So she had been right. Something *had* happened that night on the coast.

Her stepsister lit a cigarette with a hand that was still shaking so badly she could hardly get the flame near the tip. 'César said I'd never work again if I stayed in the UK. He said I was a spiteful, nasty harpy and I wasn't fit to polish your shoes, and that if I hurt you he'd be after me likc a shark in a feeding frenzy...and the worst thing is...it was *all* true!' Her face crumpling on that final wail, Petra sobbed in very real distress.

'*You slept with César...*' Dixie gulped, feeling as if she had been smacked in the face by a brick, trying to be big enough to come to terms with such a betrayal and finally doggedly forcing herself upright to offer comfort. Whatever Petra had done, César had no business intimidating her to such an extent.

'Slept with César? Chance would be a fine thing!' Petra hissed through her falling tears. 'I threw myself at him that morning in Spain and he told me to *wise up*! He wasn't even tempted. In fact, do you know what the worst thing was?'

Not even tempted? Dixie suddenly found her sympathy gushing a lot more freely and closed her arms round her much taller stepsister to bring her down on to the sofa beside her. 'No...what was the worst thing?'

'César *knew* I was going to make a pass at him and he tried to head me off, and then, when I sort of moved close...' Her stepsister's tremulous voice faltered and she burst back into tears.

'What?'

Petra emerged from her hair, looking pathetic. 'He said he got this really creepy feeling when I did that, so could I please stop it?' she howled. 'And I just felt so *ugly* and *horrible* then!'

Dixie patted her shoulder soothingly. 'I can understand that…'

'Then he left me sitting in that limo on my own most of the morning…like I was just nobody!' Petra wept. 'First he went into this jeweller's, and I'm sure he was in there an hour, and then he went into the hotel, and he was away even longer, and when he came out he was in this really freezing hostile mood and he ignored me. I was really starting to *hate* him by then—'

Dixie broke into that self-absorbed flood. 'So what did you try to blackmail César about today?'

'I called him up out of the blue this morning and told him he'd be really sorry if he didn't agree to see me,' her stepsister revealed shakily. 'And when he showed up I threatened to tell Jasper Dysart that your marriage was just a big empty nothing!'

Dixie turned pale. 'Oh dear…'

'It was my way of trying to get my own back,' her stepsister whispered shamefacedly. 'I'd never have done it. But if I ripped off some money from César, I thought I would feel better about him humiliating me!'

'I don't think César meant to humiliate you, Petra.'

'It was *very* humiliating when he burst out laughing at my threat and told me that you were pregnant!' Petra protested, shredding a tissue violently between her thin fingers. 'And then he got really cold and heavy and scary and said he'd *pay* just to get me out of your life, and I felt even worse then!'

Trying very hard not to smile, Dixie comforted her distraught stepsister. All Petra's real problems came tumbling out then. How she'd stopped getting modelling assignments in London because she was getting older. How nobody had shown the slightest interest in her bid to become an actress in Los Angeles. And Dixie finally began to see what had really been bothering Petra when she'd arrived in Spain.

'I was just so jealous. I just couldn't credit you had got hitched to this mega-rich, gorgeous guy, and there was me, trying so hard all these years and never even getting close to the altar!' Petra pointed out chokily.

'I encouraged you by telling you that our marriage was a fake—'

'It wouldn't have mattered. I was so desperate to prove myself more fanciable than you I'd *still* have tried to poach him!'

'I know,'

'He said he was going to come straight home now and tell you *everything*…so I had to get here first, because I really don't want to lose you, because you're always there for me…' Petra mumbled tightly. 'Nobody else ever is.'

At that very moment the door flew open. Petra cringed into the sofa. Dixie stood up. César got only one aggressive step into the room.

'I'm really grateful you found Petra for me, César,' Dixie delivered with a determined smile. 'And now that she's told me everything we're mending fences.'

'Mending fences?' César gritted incredulously, a fulminating toughness clenching his darkly handsome features.

'So you're a bit sort of superfluous here at the minute,' Dixie mentioned, very apologetically.

César backed off with extreme reluctance.

Dixie got Petra calmed down and tucked into a taxi.

César was waiting behind the front door for her. 'I should've been straight with you about Petra right from the start,' he announced darkly. 'The minute you said her name the night you explained about those debts, I recognised it. She's notorious! A publicity-grabbing, free-loading, prom—'

'I know,' Dixie interceded gently. 'Did you honestly think I didn't?'

César took an unusual split second to close his mouth again.

'I lived with her for quite a while,' Dixie reminded him. 'But I always try not to judge other people just because they're from a different mould. Petra's always been very insecure.'

César parted his lips, looked deep into Dixie's reproachful blue eyes and subsided again, like a volcano with a lid suddenly crammed forcibly down on its fiery destructive flow.

'I'm very fond of her and you really don't need to protect me from her. You certainly don't need to bring out any big guns. She'd never have carried out that stupid threat. She's just been going through a rough patch and her self-esteem is very low.' Dixie sighed with compassion. 'She got used to relying on her looks to get her everything she wants. Now she needs support and understanding so that she can make some changes—'

'*Accidenti!* If you think she's going to change—'

'She will, but not overnight.' Quiet confidence backed that assurance from Dixie. 'She really has no choice. She can't run around dressed like a teenage raver for ever. And it's all right. She won't want to visit when you're around,' she told him soothingly. 'She really doesn't fancy you a bit now.'

Dumbfounded by that decidedly upbeat conclusion, César watched Dixie head for the stairs.
'Where are you going?'

'I'm meeting Scott for a drink after he comes
out of work.'

César froze.

'You said it was OK.'

'I lied.' He said it so quietly Dixie almost
didn't hear him.

Dixie gazed down at him where he stood in
the hall.

César strode up to the landing and dug
clenched fists into the pockets of his well-cut
trousers. He didn't look at her. 'I really don't
want you to go,' he breathed in a ferociously taut
undertone. 'I'm scared that if you see him again
you'll realise you're still crazy about him.'

'I'm scared'. Knowing how much that admission must have cost him, Dixie just melted. 'I'll
cancel, then. You didn't need to worry,' she murmured gently. 'I've loved you to bits for weeks
now.'

Having dropped that news because she felt he
deserved it, Dixie continued on to the bedroom
to call and cancel her arrangement with Scott.
Would she regret telling César that she loved him
later? She didn't think so. It got harder and
harder to conceal her own emotions.

César followed her into the room. 'You said
you loved me…' he prompted, not quite levelly.

'Does that mean you're just sort of very *fond* of me, or that you're as keen on me as you were on Scott?'

Her heart just overflowed. He sounded so vulnerable. She turned round with a helplessly tender look on her face. 'I was just infatuated with the idea of being in love with Scott. That was only the tiniest shadow of what I feel for you.'

His strained dark eyes blazed into brilliance. 'I thought it was still Scott—'

'You pushed him out, but I didn't want to face that at first…because I didn't think we had any future.'

César reached down and took her hands and drew her to him. 'I've been praying we had a future ever since the night Jasper was taken ill.'

Dixie's eyes rounded. 'That soon? Our very first night together?'

'*Dio!* It was really weird. I just looked down at you outside the bedroom door and it was like being hit with a brick,' César imparted gruffly.

Dixie was hanging on his every word. 'Painful?' she probed worriedly.

'I'd just realised I was in love with you, and I didn't want to let go of you in case you got away,' César revealed, a dark flush emphasising his taut cheekbones. 'And then I felt terrific the next morning, until you shot me down by saying it was a mistake and how Scott was the only one for you—'

'Oh dear…I thought that was what you wanted to hear. I really did.' A sort of heavenly chorus was sounding in Dixie's bemused head at that moment. César *loved* her. He'd felt as if he had been hit with a brick, which suggested a moment of stunning self-revelation. Suddenly those words acquired the hue of a deeply romantic and touching confession.

'What I *wanted* to hear? Are you kidding?' César demanded, a full octave higher, keen to tell her just how wrong she'd been in that assessment. 'I was already sick to death of the guy's name, but that morning I wanted to wipe him off the face of the earth! Every time I turned round there he was, like an invisible presence!'

Dixie stretched up and framed his furious face with two adoring hands. 'I'm sorry I upset you like that. I wouldn't have done it for the world if I'd known how you felt about me.'

Thoroughly consoled, César seemed to recollect himself then. His stunning dark eyes shimmered. He curved his mouth into the centre of one of her palms and then he started kissing her fingers in the most shockingly erotic way, and she got all out of breath and her knees wobbled. With the sense of good timing that always distinguished him, César got the message and lifted her up into his arms.

Later, she didn't remember how they'd got to the bed, and their clothes had sort of melted away. And after they had made wild, passionate love, with the new sweet knowledge that lay between them and joined them closer than ever, they were able to talk again.

'So there I was, feeling very rejected,' César relived feelingly, back on the topic of the morning after their first intimacy.

'And you're not used to feeling rejected,' Dixie slotted in tenderly, stringing a line of little sympathetic kisses across a wide brown shoulder which tensed unexpectedly. 'So it must have really hurt.'

'You're always shooting me down out of the sky.' César turned up her face and smiled with so much love down at her. 'I was really panicking when we went out to join Jasper for lunch—'

'Panicking?' Dixie looked dubious.

'As far as I could see you were still clinging to Scott, and I wasn't going to get another opportunity to change that!' César extended ruefully. 'So when Jasper dropped the news that he was getting organised for our wedding, it was like a last-minute rescue. I reckoned the minute I got a wedding ring on your finger I'd be in a position to stage an all-out war on your affections—'

'You really wanted to marry me?' Dixie gasped, and then she recalled the rough sincerity with which he had persuaded her to go ahead and marry him, and knew she was hearing the absolute truth.

'*Per meraviglia!* Of course I did. I'd never have let Jasper push us that far if I hadn't!' César stressed. 'I could have given him two dozen different reasons why we shouldn't get married that quickly—not the least being that you deserved the chance to have the enjoyment of planning a proper wedding.'

'But it was a lovely wedding,' Dixie assured him. 'And we had a terrific honeymoon.'

'After your stepsister arrived, I couldn't get you away fast enough,' César confided, without a shade of remorse. 'One glance was enough to tell me she was out to cause trouble.'

'I didn't see that until it was too late. She told me she thought you were really attracted to her—'

'In her dreams,' César growled like a grizzly bear.

Dixie told him that Petra wasn't really as bad as he seemed to think. He didn't look madly impressed by the news, but at least he wasn't arguing any more. Some unanswered questions continued to worry at Dixie, and she was eager to make further inroads into César's wonderfully new and welcome willingness to explain his own feelings and motivations.

'So, if you were so fed up with the idea of Scott, why did you encourage me to ring him on our wedding night?'

'You just looked so lost and unhappy after getting that stupid letter he sent…' César grimaced. 'I felt guilty. I felt I didn't have the right to deny you contact with him—'

'Oh, César, if you loved me that was really sweet and unselfish of you…' Dixie's eyes misted over her view of his broodingly handsome and tense features.

'It was a buck stupid impulse!' César countered. 'And when I heard you oozing care and compassion on the phone to him I just wanted him dead and buried! So I went into the kitchen and smashed my fist against the wall and hit the blasted can opener…'

'Oh, d-dear.' Dixie's voice wobbled betrayingly in spite of her attempt to hold back her sudden amusement. 'Your poor thumb.'

'I was just eaten with jealousy.'

He had finally admitted it. She kissed his thumb in reward.

'And then after that I thought I was in with a real chance, because I never believed you were just using me for sex, *mi amore*,' César revealed, curving her close with two possessive hands and studying her with even more possessive eyes.

'No, I knew I was in love with you by then, but I didn't want to scare you off…and then I did that anyway, in Granada,' Dixie lamented.

'You really shocked me, *cara mia*,' César agreed. 'I just had to get out of the city and sort everything out in my head. Once I'd done that, I realised that I couldn't really expect you to feel any other way when I hadn't admitted how I felt about you. Then Petra arrived for breakfast and really wound me up.'

'I know…let's forget about that,' Dixie urged.

'I was coming back to the clinic to tell you that I loved you and I bought the ring on the way. I remembered you saying that rubies stood for passionate love… *What's wrong?*'

'I've really misjudged you.' Dixie sighed. 'And now I understand it all. You saw that hotel bill and knew I'd been calling Scott—'

'That shot the ground out from under me, and I was too proud to tell you how I felt then,' César admitted. 'But I'd cooled off by the time I got back to London, and I tried to keep the lines open between us. I also grovelled to Spike to get him on my side. I was ready to do anything it took to hang on to you…'

Such confessions were music to Dixie's ears. 'So the baby really was good news?'

'The *best*!' César grinned at her with wolfish satisfaction and smoothed a rather smug hand over her tummy. 'I really struck gold. I was ready to play a thousand violins about the baby needing a father.'

'I was so happy when you said you didn't want a divorce.' An expression of dismay suddenly crossed Dixie's features. 'Gosh, Bruce was trying to get hold of you to tell you that you had to call the chairman of the Osana Corporation—'

'Relax, I picked him up on the car phone.'

'Oh, no...and I've just stood poor Scott up!' Dixie registered in horror as she realised what time it was.

'Happens to the best of us. You can ask him to our wedding reception, but tell him he must bring a partner. You're very much spoken for,' César reminded her, watching her edge surreptitiously off the bed to let Spike in because he was whining piteously outside the door.

'Just for a little while...he gets awfully lonely.'

'Just like César the fish... A *fish*!' César emphasised without warning as Dixie turned, wearing a gobsmacked look. 'How could you christen a goldfish with my name?'

Sidling back into bed, Dixie breathed, 'Because he was always eating other fish. How did you find out?'

'Fisher couldn't resist letting me know. I didn't think it was really sweet either. There's comparisons and there's comparisons, and a manic goldfish—'

'No, he's got a partner now, and I think he's settling down…and you had that beautiful pond built just for him—'

'I was very tempted to stick him in with a very large and hungry carp to teach him the rules of the jungle!'

'Only you didn't.' Dixie ran an appreciative hand over his magnificent torso, feeling him tense in instantaneous response, revelling in the glow of love in his intense dark eyes, feeling she should have worked out long ago that her warmth would almost inevitably draw him to her. 'You're changing…'

'No, I'm still the cold, critical, inhuman guy you fell madly in love with,' César rushed to assert, somewhat apprehensively. 'I'm not going to change!'

'Spike, get down off this bed!' Dixie called in a shocked aside. 'He's never been allowed on a bed in his life…what's got into him?'

César looked slightly uneasy.

Dixie surveyed him in mute disbelief.

'He was crying like a baby. He was really missing you. He'd have dug compassion out of a stone!' César protested in his own defence.

Dixie concealed a tender smile against his shoulder. She just loved him to death, and he loved her, and he loved their unborn child, and he even loved her dog and tolerated her goldfish.

For a once commitment-shy male, he had made tremendous strides, and she was planning to spend the rest of her life ensuring he never had cause for a single regret.